Murder in the House

A 1920s historical mystery

A Dora and Rex Mystery
Book 7

Lynn Morrison

Marketing Chair Press

Cover design by DLR Cover Designs

Published by

The Marketing Chair Press, Oxford, England

LynnMorrisonWriter.com

Print ISBN: 978-1-917361-01-9

Contents

Cast of Characters

DORA'S HOUSEHOLD
Theodora Laurent - femme fatale
Inga Kay - companion
Harris - butler
Archie and Basil - footmen
Cynthia - housemaid

REX'S HOUSEHOLD
Lord Rex Bankes-Fernsby - spy partner
Dowager Duchess of Rockingham - grandmother
Lady Caledonia - sister

FRIENDS AND COLLEAGUES
Lord Audley - spymaster
Lord Clark Kenworthy, Earl Rivers - friend
Prudence Adams - friend

WESTMINSTER
Lord Grant McAlister
Mrs Ellen Liddell

John Smithers, MP

COMMUNISTS
Ben Bradley
Leonard Thompson
Walter Philipson
Anita Thornberry

Chapter 1
A Grisly Find

For hundreds of years, the halls of Westminster Palace had attracted visitors from around the world. Some came to appreciate the architecture or historical significance. Others came to imagine the power of the men—and now women—who cast the votes to decide the laws of the land.

Little did these visitors know that the true power lay not in the spaces that formed the public domain, but in the meeting rooms and private offices open only by invitation.

In one such meeting room, eleven distinguished men sat around a table. Beneath the polished surface, the table bore the signs of its age in faint scratches and nicks. So, too, did the men around it. The grey strands in their hair and lined faces were a testament to their years shouldering the fate of a nation.

Of this group, one man stood apart—Lord Clark Kenworthy. The nameplate before him declared him as Earl Rivers, though it still gave him a start every time he read it. Earl Rivers was his father, or he had been until a mere three months earlier. A winter chill had settled deep into the man's bones. Lord Clark had rung in the new year at his father's side. Two days later, the earl was gone, and Lord Clark found himself bearing his father's title and the responsibilities that came with it.

"Rivers? Rivers?" The man repeated Clark's title until Clark's head snapped up. "I'd be interested in hearing your thoughts on this matter. After all, it will be your generation who will bear the cost if we choose wrong."

Clark fought the urge to lounge back in his chair or to make a flippant reply. That was the old Clark—the bright young thing who organised elaborate scavenger hunts and stayed out until dawn. Now he was Earl Rivers, member of important subcommittees, and Lord Audley's protégé.

That was likely why Lord Audley had just called on him to share his opinion. Thankfully, Clark had not been so lost in thought to have missed the discussion topic.

"You may think me inexperienced, but on the matter of workers' rights, we would be fools to ignore the government's responsibilities. There are plenty of foreign foes who welcome the chance to sow the seeds of chaos. I believe our best defence is to co-opt elements of their platform. Men and women will be less likely to join the communists if someone else is listening to their voices."

Several men in the room harrumphed in disagreement, but more still had thoughtful expressions. Lord Audley nodded his approval. Lord McAlister, the current leader of the House of Lords, took up the baton and continued the conversation. Clark's gaze slipped to the young men seated along the back wall, landing on the dark-haired, fresh-faced chap in the middle. Leonard Thompson was in his second month of clerking for McAlister. His hand flew across his paper as he kept the minutes of the meeting. Clark hoped he had put a star next to his own words. After all, Clark had aimed them at Leonard's ears.

Leonard was no ordinary clerk. Unlike the men to his left

and right, he had not spent hours campaigning during the last election. Not for McAlister's party, anyway.

Leonard's presence in the room was by design and not by right. Unassuming though he was, he was the lynchpin in a plan known to only four people in the world. It still boggled Clark's mind that he was one of them. If secrets were the currency of Westminster, Clark was now a very wealthy man. Like everything else, he kept that information to himself.

The meeting rolled on for another two hours, bringing the group to no consensus on what to do about the plight of England's working class or the communists who threatened disorder. It was a topic far too complex to be settled in a day, or week, or even a month.

Unless someone brought the matter to a head.

"Rivers, can I offer you a drink before you head home?" Lord Audley asked.

Clark fell into step at Audley's side. Though there were few people left so long after the regular working day, they all moved aside in deference to Lord Audley.

"They respect you, too," Audley murmured as they walked. The only thing more frightening than Audley's intellect was his seeming ability to read Clark's mind. "It is your body language that gives you away," Audley explained once they reached the privacy of his office.

He poured them each a finger of amber-coloured Scotch from a crystal decanter. "Ask Dora to give you some pointers on how to wear a mask to hide your true sentiments. She did well enough in training Rex."

The image of the gorgeous vixen, laughing as she fluffed her red-blonde curls, sprang to mind. Femme fatale, spy, and former English debutante. "If Dora's family lineage was not readily available in Debrett's, I would wonder if she was a witch with a magic wand," Clark countered.

3

"Do not give her any ideas," Audley groaned. "She is hard enough to manage as she is. She is fully human, with a similar background to your own. If she can fool the whole world, she can teach you how to display self-confidence. Well-earned confidence," Audley added. "Your reply in the meeting today was excellent. I noticed many heads around the room nodding in agreement."

Clark's cheeks flushed, but it was not because of the Scotch he had gulped down. Audley meant his words. Clark almost believed them. He had made significant progress in his transition from a bored, wealthy lad to a serious statesman.

But until he had pulled off a plan of his own and proved to them both he was worthy of the title of future spymaster, Clark would suffer from moments of self-doubt.

"Are you ready to tell me about whatever it is you and McAlister are planning? Do not deny that you two have met several times recently. Lord Cavendish has been complaining about it."

Clark gulped. "I hope he has not given you too much trouble on my account."

Audley waved him off. "Given how rarely Dora's father and I see eye-to-eye, if he is annoyed, you must be doing something right."

"He is annoyed because I am currently backing the Labour horse instead of his beloved Tories."

"That is true," Audley agreed with a chuckle. "But that does not shed any light on your plans. What are you and McAlister planning? And when will you let me in on the secret?"

Clark resisted the urge to give in to Lord Audley's weighty gaze. The first lesson he had learned was to hold his cards close to his chest, even from Lord Audley. "I will report in at the appropriate time. For now, suffice it to say that I am simply supporting the man's efforts to shore up his new majority."

Clark tossed back the last of his Scotch and rose from his chair. "I still have piles of papers waiting on my desk. Was there anything else you needed?"

Lord Audley shook his head and told Clark to have a good evening. "I applaud you for standing up to even me. I have full faith in your abilities. Get some rest, and I do not mean by laying your head on your desk. We have a full day again tomorrow."

Now on his own, Clark acknowledged people as they passed, most on their way out of the building. He called each one by their name and took pride in their surprise that he knew who they were. If he had one superpower, it was storing names and faces. He had long considered it a game and pulled it out like a parlour trick.

"How can you remember them all?" his friends would ask.

He always shrugged his shoulders, preferring silence to telling the truth.

Clark's memory functioned like a vast web, woven with spider threads, him at the centre of it all. Any time he met someone new, his mind spun a thread to connect them somewhere else.

Rex, dear friend though he was, would think him crazy. Dora, however, was likely to understand and, more importantly, appreciate this skill.

At his desk, Clark turned the pages of meeting minutes one by one, identifying which political alliances remained strong and which allies were pulling apart. He read until the words blurred on the page.

It was past midnight. The witching hour had come and gone on silent feet. He restored his papers to some semblance of order and tossed the crumb-crusted sandwich wrapper into the bin.

Clark chose the long way around the building, taking his time to read the names on the doorways of the other offices. He passed party meeting rooms, libraries, storage cupboards that sometimes functioned as confessionals. He smiled at the memory of the time he found Dora and Rex hiding in one. How had he overlooked all the signs of their undercover activities for so long?

Because they made it easy for people to underestimate them, he reminded himself. He, too, could have chosen that path. But he valued respect, especially now that he held his family's title. Respect would open many closed doors, and better enable him to do his part for the nation.

And so he worked late into the night on most evenings. When his mind was so full of ideas and questions that he could no longer focus, he walked through the halls. Tonight, it wasn't confusion that bothered him so much as concern. His plan with McAlister had to come off without a hitch. He wished he could check in on the man, though he was almost certainly long gone. Nonetheless, Clark turned left at the next corridor and directed his steps toward McAlister's office. To his surprise, light spilled from beneath the door.

Clark stopped and gave a light rap. No one answered. He knocked again, louder this time. He waited a beat and then tried the handle. It turned in his hand.

The outer office was dimly lit by a single desk lamp, casting long shadows across the room. The air hung heavy with the lingering scent of tobacco and leather-bound books. Moonlight filtered through the tall windows, illuminating dust motes that danced in the still air. The clerk's desk had letters stacked to one side. A faint white powdery smear marred the leather blotter. The chair was pushed back as though waiting for its occupant's return.

The door to the House leader's inner sanctum stood ajar.

Clark nudged it open further. Rich mahogany panelling adorned the walls, interspersed with portraits of stern-faced

6

politicians from ages past. A massive oak desk dominated the room, its surface a landscape of papers, folders, and leather-bound tomes. The green-shaded desk lamp cast an eerie glow across the room, creating pockets of shadow in the corners.

As Clark's eyes adjusted to the dim light, he caught sight of something out of place. Near the desk lay a dark shape on the luxurious Persian carpet. His breath caught in his throat as he realised it was a man lying face down, one arm outstretched, as if reaching for help.

He hurried forward, the thick carpet muffling his footfall. The prone figure remained motionless. As he drew closer, a sense of disquiet mounted in his chest. With each step, the grim reality of the situation became clearer, and Clark knew that his discovery would change everything.

Chapter 2
Rex Answers the Call

Not too far away in a Belgravia mansion on a well-respected street, an orange marmalade cat leapt onto a wide bed in a dark bedroom.

The cat padded over the covers, not taking any care to avoid the splayed limbs lying underneath. When the cat judged himself to be at the appropriate place, he leapt forward, sinking light sharp claws into the person-shaped mound.

Lord Reginald Bankes-Fernsby, known to all as Lord Rex, jolted into awareness with a certainty he had been stabbed in the buttocks. He fumbled under the pillow, searching for a weapon, until a plaintive meow stopped him.

"Mews?" Rex asked.

A furry head bumped against his shoulder. Rex swatted him away. Mews retaliated with another meow. "Darling, do something about that cat of yours... or I will," Dora threatened in a harsh whisper.

Rex kissed his wife's forehead and got up to see what the cat wanted. He did not bother with his dressing gown, but he slid his feet into his slippers.

When he got to the hallway, he heard a faint trill coming from downstairs.

"Who is ringing at this hour?" he asked the cat. Mews's only reply was to nearly trip him on his way down the stairs. Rex lifted the earpiece and croaked a hello into the phone.

"Rex, old chap, so glad I caught you," a familiar voice echoed over the line.

"Woke me, more like it. Why are you ringing so late, Clark? Did we have plans?"

On the other end of the line, Clark laughed. Rex had spent enough time with him to recognise the solemn edge to the chuckle. Rex wiped the sleep from his blurry eyes, suddenly wide awake.

"You did indeed forget. I considered letting you get your beauty rest, but this latest escapade of mine is too good for you to miss."

"Escapade?" Rex queried.

"Yes, and you are already behind. Meet me at the W and I'll bring you up to speed." Clark paused and then added, "Oh Rex, bring along a couple of pairs of leather gloves and silk scarves."

"What?" Rex asked, but he was talking to thin air. Clark had rung off. He replaced the phone on the credenza and hurried back to his room, taking the steps two at a time.

The cat had already claimed his space in the bed. Rex circled the bed to where his wife was sleeping. He leaned close and whispered to Dora that he had to dash out to meet Clark.

"Do you want me to come?" she asked, sleep heavy in her voice.

"No need. He said to come to Westminster and did not ask me to bring anyone else along."

"Fine, but I expect you to tell me everything tomorrow."

Outside, Rex eschewed his Rolls-Royce for the black Model T. He attracted no attention while driving through London's quiet streets, nor when he parked near a side entrance to Parliament.

Clark opened the building door and motioned for him to keep quiet. He led the way, forcing Rex to play silent guessing games.

The halls of Westminster provoked a certain level of seriousness. Though the halls had witnessed their share of arguments, heated and otherwise, the ornate designs encouraged guests to hold their tongues. This was a working palace, ruled by elected and appointed men and women.

Clark was one of these privileged individuals. His steady pace ate up the floor. His shoulders, however, were ramrod straight, and his hands coiled against his sides. He stopped only once, in a dark alcove, waiting for a guard to pass.

Rex tried to think of the last time he had seen Clark so tense. The man's insouciance was practically infamous. When tensions ballooned, Clark was the pin to pop them. He would tell a joke, usually at his own expense, and everyone would laugh.

Tonight, Clark was going out of his way to avoid people. Again and again, the men stepped out of sight to hide from guards walking their routes. Clark fanned his fingers and shook his arms, then balled his hands into fists again.

The only time Rex could recall Clark acting this way was the time Rex had discovered him standing over a body. Rex quashed that thought. They were in Parliament, and, more importantly, not in the middle of a secret mission.

Clark finally stopped outside the door to the office of the leader of the House of Lords. He pulled out a key and unlocked the entrance. When Rex had come inside, Clark locked it behind them.

Clark did not stop there. He kept going into the inner office, where he leaned sideways, as if searching for something, and he must have found the object in question, because Rex could hear him heave a sigh of relief.

"Are you going to tell me now what is going on?" Rex asked.

"I need your help."

"Of course. With what?"

"Moving a body."

Rex grabbed hold of the back of the nearest chair, waiting for his confusion to clear. "Body? Whose body?"

Rather than answer, Clark stepped aside to allow Rex to enter the other room.

Rex was no stranger to death, but he was far from a ghoul. His slow steps brought him closer, though his mind begged him to reconsider his actions.

Just as Clark had said, there was a body lying on the Turkish carpet. The only positive was that it was not the body of the leader of the House. Though facedown, Rex noted right away that the hair colour was wrong.

"I did not kill him."

Rex spun around and gaped at his friend. "I did not think that you had. But perhaps you could explain why you need to carry this man's body out of Westminster Palace, and what gloves and scarves have to do with it."

"Come," Clark said, motioning for Rex to return to the outer chamber. He pointed toward the simple wooden desk set aside for a clerk or private secretary. "Do you see this?"

"The white smear? What is it?" Rex leaned over to inspect it, but Clark pulled him back.

"I suspect it is some sort of poison."

Rex jerked sideways. "Start at the beginning."

"We don't have time for me to explain everything. I will give you the key points now, as I would like your judgement on the situation. The rest I will tell you once we are outside of this building."

"Fair enough." Rex waved his hand to cede the floor.

"The dead man's name is Leonard Thompson. He is McAlister's new clerk. Well, let's just say I helped him get his job. I worked late and noticed McAlister's light was still on when I left. I came in and found the scene just as you see it."

Rex scanned the room. "Did you call me from here?"

"No. I hurried back to my office."

"Did you touch anything?"

"Only the man's carotid, to confirm he was dead."

Rex nodded in approval. "Let's move on to the cause of death."

"This is Leonard's desk. Based on what I can see, it appears he was sorting through McAlister's mail. I believe the white powder you see came from one of the letters. Leonard tried to dust it off the blotter and got it onto his hands. He got up, went into McAlister's office to look for something, and died there. Now, you look and give me your assessment."

Rex's mind shifted into analytical mode as he adopted the single-minded focus he used for his spy missions with Dora. The pile of correspondence, some matched with typed replies, aligned with what Clark had said. In addition to the obvious smear, there was a faint sprinkling of white dust across some of the letters.

Rex moved into the inner office once again—all the way in this time, not stopping until he reached the far wall. From there, he could see the top desk drawer was partially open. McAlister's diary sat on the desk, flipped open to the current month.

The poor clerk must have stumbled or fallen over as a pen pot lay on its side. A few loose pens had rolled across the desk while another was on the floor.

"Which letter contained the poison?"

"I am not positive. Look there, near his arm. You can see the edge of another paper."

12

Sure enough, the wrinkled edge of the paper peeked out. Rex had mistaken it for a pattern in the carpet weave at first glance.

"I cannot find any reason to doubt your guess. What I still do not understand is why we need to move the body."

"We must make it look like he died while working at his own desk, and not in here. The police detectives must think the poison came in a letter addressed to the leader of the House of Lords."

"Do you have reason to believe it might not have?"

Clark frowned. "I will not know for sure until we move the body. I did not want to risk getting any of the poison on myself."

"Thus the request for gloves and scarves..." Rex opened his coat and retrieved the items from his inner pocket.

After the men pulled on the gloves and wrapped the scarves over their mouths and noses, they set to their task. Rex took the man's arms, leaving Clark to take his feet. The man's hands bore faint traces of powder, while the thumb of his right hand was perfectly clean.

They frog-marched their way through the doorway, taking great care not to bump against it. It took a moment of discussion to agree on the best way to position the body. Rex added the finishing touches, knocking over the desk's pen pot.

Before he moved on to scattering the pile of letters, a thought crossed his mind. *Where was the envelope?* Rex flicked through the discards in the bin but found nothing that stood out as unusual.

Clark urged him to hurry. "A guard could decide to check why the light is still on. Quick, pass me a couple of the opened letters." Rex handed the top two over and Clark wedged them under the dead man.

All that was left was to restore the inner office back to how it should have been.

Rex collected the loose pens and smoothed the carpet fibres into place. He stayed away from the piece of paper out of concern it might be the source of the poison. Clark took care of the diary, using his handkerchief to dust off the pages and to wipe the outside before returning it to the drawer. He used the last of a pitcher of water to make doubly sure there were no traces of poison in the leader's inner sanctum.

Soon, only the abandoned sheet of paper remained on the floor. Rex fetched an empty envelope from the cupboard and offered it to Clark. Wearing gloves and holding his handkerchief, Clark gently flipped the paper right side up.

Based on Clark's expression alone, Rex was certain the man was unhappy with what he saw. Clark did not offer any explanation. He lifted the paper by its edge and slid it into the waiting envelope.

"What now? Will you phone the police?"

Clark raised his hand to rub the back of his neck, but caught himself before he touched his skin. "No, although it pains me to say that. It is best for everyone that someone else makes this discovery."

They pilfered an old newspaper from another room to wrap around their gloves and Clark's handkerchief, and then tossed them into a bin in another room. Rex kept the scarves, since they belonged to Dora. She could make the decision of what to do with them.

"I will follow you home," Clark said when they made it safely outside.

"No, go home and get some sleep. We cannot do anything about this until morning, right?"

Clark gave a mournful shake of his head. "I doubt sleep will come, though I would welcome the escape from this madness. But you are right. I will come round mid-morning."

Chapter 3
Dora Argues her Case

Dora bit back a laugh when her husband came stumbling into the dining room the next morning. His pale blond hair stuck up one side, and he had a crease marking his cheek. He scrubbed his face and then dropped into his chair.

"Why didn't you wake me?" he asked, though there was no heat in his tone.

"I was not sure what time you came home. I figured it must have been late since you slept on the sofa rather than risk waking me."

"Waking you was not the issue. Mews was stretched along the length of my side of the bed. When I attempted to move him, he bit me." Rex held out his hand to show a red scratch.

"Looks like he did more than just bite," Dora countered. "You had better put some cream on that. It looks terrible."

Dora's dear companion Inga strode into the dining room, followed closely by her husband Harris. "I see Sleeping Beauty is awake." She took her seat and pointed her husband toward the pot of coffee. "You had best pour Rex a cup first."

Harris poured two cups and placed them both in front of

Rex. "Drink these both and then catch us up on whatever is going on."

"All I know is that Clark is involved." Dora wiggled her eyebrows. "That could mean anything, knowing Clark's penchant for antics."

"Come now, Dora," Inga chastised. "The poor man has turned a new leaf."

Dora propped her chin on her hand and pretended to pout. "That's a pity. I'm loath to admit it, but the man has become boring."

"Only if you count moving a body as boring," Rex grumbled into his coffee cup.

Harris choked on a bite of toast, causing Inga to have to pat him on the back.

"I hope there is an explanation coming soon," Dora warned her husband, "because you cannot leave a sentence like that hanging in the air."

Dora's exasperation had to wait. Just then, the trill of the doorbell echoed from the corridor. Harris got up to answer it and returned with the man of the hour.

Clark was even worse off than Rex. Deep purple shadows hung beneath his bloodshot eyes, marring his otherwise handsome face. Even his meticulously groomed moustache, normally a point of pride, drooped pathetically at the corners, mirroring his stressed demeanour. The man had aged years overnight, with worry lines etching themselves prematurely across his forehead and around his mouth.

Dora took one look at him and skipped right past hello, going straight in with her questions.

"Did you really call Rex to come help you move a body?"

"Only into the next room," Clark replied in a droll tone.

Harris took another cup from the sideboard and filled it nearly to the brim. "Drink some coffee and try again."

It took coffee and a full plate of food for the men to recover their normal wit. After the footmen Archie and Basil cleared the plates from the table, the team got down to business.

"Although you all have questions about last night, it will only make sense if I start at the beginning." Clark waited for the group to nod in understanding. He continued, "I contrived a plan, together with Grant McAlister, to undermine any challenges to the Labour government that might come from the left."

"The communists, you mean," Dora clarified.

"Just so. Like Lord Audley, I believe that our government works best when we have a healthy opposition party. Labour leads a minority government. I believe the Tories only agreed to give them control so that they would fail. Lately, the Tories have preferred to play up the communist threat rather than argue against Labour's policies. Giving the Commies space in the headlines gives credence to the Russian ideology. I am sure you do not need me to explain why that is bad."

"Indeed not. Inga and I attended the Second World Congress of the Third International in Moscow back in 1920 and got an earful of their plans. It is not that all their sentiments are wrong, but I doubt causing the fall of the government is the best hope for our future. At least, not our future here in England."

"Hear, hear," Clark said. "I took it upon myself to come up with a way to put all talk of the commies to rest, but short of rounding them all up and shoving them behind bars, I could find no foolproof way. But then, your father gave me an idea."

"My father?" Dora's mouth dropped open. "Surely you did not get his help with this."

"Not wittingly." A sly grin crossed Clark's face. "He blathered on and on one day about how the Labour party and the commies would join forces to push this country into ruin.

17

After a few times of being reminded about their common ground, I thought, why not exploit that?"

Inga raised a hand to halt Clark there. "How would that neutralise the Russians?"

"Lord Cavendish expects the two groups to work as equals, with Russia feeding instructions to their side of the equation. I foresaw a different partnership, one where each side achieved their aims—or at least some of them."

As Clark laid out his original plan in full, Dora could not help but be impressed by how far he had come in the last six months. To the rest of the world, his transition into a serious political player had been gradual. Only a special few had seen how hard he had worked to remedy the deficiencies in his knowledge.

The man had burnt the candle at both ends, studying all day and then going out to parties. There, he gradually let more political talk slip into his conversations.

To their group of acquaintances, it was as though Clark was gripped by a fever. Rather than think him a bore, they found his almost childlike enthusiasm endearing. Whoever had taken part in one of his elaborate hunts about town knew of his intelligence.

With Dora and Rex looking on, Clark had turned the latest goings-on at Westminster into thrilling tales of secret alliances, moves, and countermoves. A few of their friends had even gone so far as to vote in the last election.

The members of the House of Lords had proved to be a much harder audience to sway. Lord Audley told Clark that he had to get up on his feet on his own. If he needed Audley's help to gain the other lords' respect, he was doomed.

Clark understood the assignment, but he found another way to accomplish his goal. No one in Westminster was going to buy his sudden interest, not after he spent so long running from his responsibilities. So, he charmed them.

It was a lucky thing for the world that she had not lost her heart to Clark, Dora thought to herself. The combination of her feminine wiles and Clark's beguiling charm would have led to them gaining domination.

Many underestimated the power of a charm offensive. Lord Audley certainly had. He had chastised Clark for spending too much time in the Lord's Dining Room and too little reading policy papers. But Clark had proven him wrong. He had wormed his way into the hearts of those men by making them view him the same way they did the newest litter of puppies from their favourite hunting dog.

And then, Clark's father had died, and the mantle of responsibility latched onto him, gripping onto his neck and wrists like manacles. Clark kept a smile on his face, but it never rose to his eyes.

Dora sought Lord Audley and begged him to step in. Her mentor promised he would, if it came to that, but he had full faith all would work out as it should. And it had until now. Until Clark's grand plan wound up dead in a Westminster office. This was a serious setback.

Now was not the time for woolgathering, not if Dora was going to help Clark find out what had gone awry. She pulled her attention back to the present and focused on Clark's explanation. Clark was sitting straighter in his chair, reminding them all why he was training to become Lord Audley's replacement.

"My plan was a long game, I admit. But given Labour has a full term ahead of it, I saw no point in rushing things. My goal was simple—to show the communists they could better serve the men and women of England by supporting a Labour government rather than bringing it down. The clerk, Leonard Thompson, was the first step."

"You got Leonard the job clerking for McAlister?" Rex asked.

"Yes, and no. I got McAlister to agree to give the man a chance to see, from up close, what Labour intends to do. The Communist leader is the one who selected Leonard. Leonard was to be the go-between."

Harris, who had sat silently up to that point, interrupted Clark. "Do you mean to tell us you, Clark Kenworthy, took a wild hare of a plan and managed to convince not one, but two major opposing politicians to work together in secret?"

"Yes." Clark nodded.

Harris slapped his knee and blurted, "My word, old boy, you deserve an OBE for your service to the nation!"

Dora agreed with Harris's sentiments.

Shaking his head with regret, Clark confessed, "I killed a man. If not with my bare hands, then with my thoughts and deeds."

"How can you say that?" Rex intervened. "You had nothing to do with poisoning him. It was some random letter."

Clark gave a morose shake of his head. "Since sleep refused to come anyhow, I took a closer look at the paper we found under Leonard's body. It was written in some kind of strange code, and I don't mean the kind we need your sister Caledonia to decipher. Frankly, it reads like one of Prudence's ridiculous gossip columns, with all the names and locations given funny names."

Dora tapped her fingers on her armrest as she considered the possible implications. "Either someone was in on Leonard's true purpose—"

"—Or it was someone from within the Communist party sending the rest of us a message," Clark finished.

Harris whistled. "That is one hell of a message."

"Indeed." Clark opened his hands and laid them wide. "The question is what do we do now?"

Rex shrugged. "You tell us. You know all the players."

"Being the one who got us into this. I need you to help me figure this out."

Rex's stance softened in the face of his friend's hesitation. "Hmm, well, I guess we should speak with McAlister."

While Dora could see the merits of Rex's suggestion, she had a different opinion. "We must talk to the Communist leader straight away. If this is a commie plot, he will have to help us stop it."

"What if he is behind the plot?" Harris asked. "You should not reveal what you know."

"It could just as well be someone on the Labour side. Or the Tories," Inga countered.

"This is why we must be methodical in our approach," Rex said, waving his hands to stop the arguments.

Dora stood to place a hand on Clark's shoulder. Rex reached for her arm when she passed. "Darling, we have forgotten a very important point."

Dora's mind raced, but so many thoughts fought for prominence that she could not guess which he referenced.

Rex turned away from Dora and directed his words at his friend. "Given how we left things in Westminster, the police and everyone else will assume McAlister was the target. We must tell him otherwise."

Chapter 4
A Friend Lends an Ear

Rex and Clark climbed into the shiny Rolls-Royce waiting out front. For once, neither man took a moment to appreciate the sleek lines of the newest model, nor did they comment on the luxurious interior. Clark remained remarkably tight-lipped, a fact that caused Rex some concern.

Rex gave a soft cough to break the tension. "Would you like to plan what we will say to Lord McAlister?"

Clark waved off Rex's offer. "What can we tell him but the truth?"

In Rex's experience with such situations, the truth was often the last thing to discuss. He supposed that would be the case when Clark and Dora met with the communists. McAlister, however, was as much on the inside of this plan as Rex. More so, perhaps, since he had been involved from the start.

If finding the right words was not what was bothering Clark, what was?

With Clark's driver behind the wheel, Rex had plenty of time to study his friend. Clark stared straight forward, but Rex was willing to bet he did not see the road or the passing cars. The shadows under Clark's eyes and the haggard droop of his moustache emphasised his anxious expression. "Penny for your thoughts, Clark," Rex said.

"Keep your money, old boy, for they are the stuff of nightmares. Every time I close my eyes, I see... well, you saw it as well. I may not have done the deed, but I might as well have put the weapon in the killer's hand."

"I disagree. You did not make this plan in isolation."

"Maybe not, but it is my responsibility to think through every outcome and come up with mitigations." Clark drew a deep breath and huffed it out in a long sigh.

"You are wrong, my friend, for no mere mortal could take on the task you described."

"Audley can," Clark countered, referencing the spymaster who served as their mentor.

"Audley has been caught wrong-footed as much as the rest of us. I can list a handful of examples if you'd like, but you have been there for most of them. You must stop beating yourself up."

Clark slumped in his seat and hung his head. "I guess I would rather chastise myself than deal with the other thoughts running through my mind."

At that pronouncement, Rex raised his eyebrows.

"Leonard reminded me of myself. Of the two of us. Not how we are, but how we might have been had we not gone to war."

"Before we forced ourselves to stop caring so much?" Rex asked gently.

Clark lifted his head and unleashed a wry grin. "Just so. He had such passion for his beliefs. Such drive and determination. He truly felt he could change the world. I envied him that."

Those who had not served on the front lines saw only the death and obvious injuries. Rex and Clark bore the invisible scars: the loss of their ideals, their innocence, and their faith in the goodness of man. The entire world had slipped into a savage madness. What was to stop it from happening again?

Of course, this was exactly the reason Lord Audley had fielded his team of spies. Clark, too, was learning the fine art of foreign diplomacy. And young men like Leonard played their parts. They owed it to him to uncover the truth about who ended his life.

As Rex and Clark approached Westminster Palace, the iconic Gothic Revival architecture loomed before them, its sand-coloured limestone façade gleaming in the late morning light. The Victoria Tower stood proudly at one end, while the famous Clock Tower housing Big Ben dominated the other. The intricate stonework and countless pinnacles created a striking silhouette against the pale spring sky.

On the pavement, a diverse array of Londoners bustled about their day. Smartly dressed clerks and civil servants hurried towards the entrance, briefcases in hand. A group of suffragettes stood nearby, their placards demanding further reforms despite the recent extension of voting rights to women. Tourists, easily identified by their wide-eyed wonder and guidebooks, snapped photographs with their Leica cameras.

For a change, Clark directed Rex toward the public entrance of the grand halls of Parliament. A pair of guards stood watch at the gate, their expressions particularly dour. The elder of the two called Clark's name as they approached.

"Lord Rivers, all sessions and committee meetings are cancelled this morning."

"Oh?" Clark replied, feigning ignorance. "How so? Is aught amiss?"

"There was a death overnight, a young clerk in the Lords' leader's office."

"In McAlister's office? That's terrible. We are actually on our way to see him. Is he here?"

"Arrived about an hour ago, my lord. As to whether he will see you, I couldn't say."

"We will go find out. At a minimum, we can pay our respects and offer our condolences." Clark thanked the guard for letting them know, and then the men continued on their way.

Westminster Hall was the oldest part of Westminster Palace, dating back to 1097. It played a significant role in British history, hosting coronation feasts, state trials, and lying-in-state ceremonies for monarchs and important figures. Such events, however, were far from the minds of Clark and Rex.

On this day, its stone walls and grand scale created an awe-inspiring atmosphere for the small groups of public visitors, mostly well-dressed middle-class citizens and the occasional curious tourist. They spoke in hushed tones, necks craned upward to admire the horizontal trusses of the Gothic hammer-beam roof or peering at the plaques marking historical events. Clark and Rex did not stop to speak with any of them as they hurried through, their quick strides echoing in the vast space as they moved through the hall.

Outside Clark's office, Clark flagged a passing secretary and asked her to deliver a message to McAlister and await a reply. Instead of returning with a note, she brought along the man himself.

McAlister entered the room, his imposing figure filling the doorway. Standing at just over six feet tall, he cut a striking figure despite his current distress. His thick mane of silver-grey hair, usually neatly combed back, was slightly tousled, with a few strands falling across his high forehead. His square-jawed face bore the ruddy complexion of an Englishman who spent his youth outdoors.

There was no sign of McAlister's affable reputation. Much like Clark, the man's shoulders were stooped and his mouth pressed together into a bloodless line. He halted at the sight of Rex sitting in the other chair, but Clark waved him in.

"We heard what happened."

Clark rose to pour the man a drink, for it appeared he could use one, but McAlister gave a shake of his head.

"Though the respite would be welcome, I dare not dull my wits. My staff are devastated, and so am I, truth be told. The detectives say he was poisoned by a letter addressed to me. In my head, I know I am not at fault, but my heart bleeds for the loss of one so young."

Clark took a deep breath and launched into the truth of what had really happened. "The letter was not addressed to you."

"It must have been. I saw the pile of correspondence." McAlister stopped then as the implications of Clark's statement set in. "What do you know of this, and who is keeping it from me?"

"I was the first to find Leonard's body—late last night, long after everyone else was gone."

McAlister's face went through a sea change of emotions at Clark's reply, as he rocked back and then half-rose to stand. For his part, Clark's stern expression never shifted. The House leader tamped down his anger and finally settled back into his chair. He rubbed his forehead and grimaced in pain. "Perhaps I will have that drink after all. Just a finger, mind you, and top it with water."

Clark fixed three glasses and handed them to the other men before taking his glass back to his seat behind the desk. McAlister held his glass in his hands but did not take a sip. "What happened? How bad is the situation? And why are you here, Lord Rex?"

Clark answered. "Rex is a trusted friend. I have called him in to help, but to explain why, I had best start at the beginning."

In a tone lacking any emotion, Clark recounted their movements the previous evening. When he got to the part about moving Leonard's body, McAlister's eyes nearly popped out of his head.

"Are you mad? You must be, to do something like that. And you?" McAlister asked, turning Rex's way. "You went along with this? Without asking any questions?"

"Suffice it to say that this is not the first time I have been called in to help the government with a sticky situation. You may trust in my complete discretion in the matter, and in my help getting to the bottom of this."

McAlister tossed back the rest of his drink and then pressed the cool crystal against his forehead. "I won't ask any more questions about your part, for I can see I will not get any answers. Tell me the rest of what you found. How did the poison get into my office?"

"We found a letter under Leonard's body. It read like a fictitious spy note, but clearly, Leonard believed it was genuine enough. It was signed with a codename," Clark added.

"The communists?" McAlister asked.

"That is our assumption. You can see now why we acted as we did. We do not want to make Leonard's, and therefore your, connection to the communist party public. We rearranged the scene to make it appear that you were the target."

"Why would the communists kill their own?"

Clark shrugged. "That is what we intend to find out."

"You can't mean to tell the communist leader about what you did. He will use it against you!"

Clark grimaced. Rex jumped in before the situation degraded any further. "We will handle the situation with care, telling everyone the bare minimum. As far as the world is concerned, Leonard died from a poisoned letter addressed to your office. The police investigation will proceed along those lines. Our conversations will be informal and precautionary. Given why Leonard was working for you, we would be remiss to not at least consider the possibility he was the target."

"Especially since he was," McAlister grumbled. "I have no choice in this matter, do I?"

"None of us do," Clark said.

McAlister set his glass on the table and stood. Before he left, he stopped to utter one last instruction. "This whole thing was your idea. If you don't make this right, you can find out what it's like to live knowing you alone brought down the government." The slam of the door behind him made both Rex and Clark flinch.

"What are we going to do, Rex?"

"What we agreed. We will find out why Leonard is dead and ensure the responsible are punished."

Clark seemed mollified by Rex's assurance. Across the desk, Rex wished he felt the same. Investigating a murder was bad enough. If Clark lost his newfound confidence in the process, it would be a tragedy of epic proportions.

Chapter 5
Ringing an Old Friend

B ack in Belgravia, Dora was putting her own plan into action. No sooner had the men departed than she sprang from the sofa and headed toward the telephone.

"Inga dear, how soon can you be ready to go?" she asked as she passed her best friend.

"That depends on where we are going. If the answer is Buckingham Palace, I will require more time than usual."

Dora turned around and propped her hand on her hip. "I am disappointed in you. You have long held the ability to predict my movements. Don't tell me you are going soft!"

"Nothing of the sort. I was merely checking to see if you still appreciate my skills. You are going to ring Sylvia. If she is free, I am already dressed for the day and can depart whenever you want."

Dora wagged a finger at Inga for playing a trick on her. In truth, she was relieved that at least something was right in her world. The day the pair of them ceased their banter would be when one of them was lying in a coffin. If it were up to Dora, she would find a way for them to carry on into the afterlife.

In her travels around the world, Dora had made a point of

cultivating friendships with interesting women. Sylvia Pankhurst certainly fit the bill. Luck was with Dora that day as she found Sylvia at home. Sylvia was delighted to hear from Dora and insisted she come straight over.

Born into a family of suffragettes, Sylvia was destined for a future in social activism. Dora had followed her activities in the news with wide eyes and great interest, from Sylvia's travels across the UK and USA to take part in women-led labour activism, to her eventual embrace of communism.

Dora drove societal change in her own small way, and it was inevitable that their paths would eventually cross. It happened after the war, when Dora found herself in Moscow for a communist congress. Sylvia had also been in attendance, and the two women had no trouble finding common ground, especially once Dora let her admiration for Sylvia show.

A frisson of excitement ran along Dora's spine as she walked into her bedroom. She dressed down for the occasion, well, down for her. She donned a pair of wide-leg wool trousers and a new silk blouse that brought out the colour of her green eyes. A brightly coloured scarf—not one of the ones Rex used for his late-night foray to Westminster—added a pop of fancy to an otherwise sedate choice of clothing. With a black felt cloche on her head, she and Inga set off.

Sylvia welcomed them into her home with open arms. "If I had a penny for every time I've seen your photograph or read your name in the paper, I could feed the world's hungry."

"Well, I do try," Dora confessed, making the other woman laugh. "You remember Inga Kay, my dear companion?"

"Of course, I do. I remember your wit as well," Sylvia replied, offering Inga her hand. "It was a bright spot when we were surrounded by so many stern Russians. Please, take a seat and tell me what brings you to darken my doorstep."

Dora and Inga had agreed on their strategy on the ride over.

Dora would begin with a fishing expedition and only delve deeper if she judged it appropriate.

"A friend of mine has had some dealings with Ben Bradley. I would like to hear your opinion of the man. I dare not ask anyone else, for they'll equate communist as evil and give me a skewed opinion."

Sylvia arched an eyebrow. "Given how much time you spend with the lords and ladies of the land, I am surprised you don't view that as a negative."

"I have always kept an open mind, as you well know. Now, tell me about him."

Sylvia studied Dora's face, searching for any hint of treachery. Dora did not take it personally. Sylvia had spent so much of her life fighting for societal change that she was right to be wary about who she trusted. She must have liked what she saw in Dora's expression, for she relaxed in her chair and gave a reply.

"How much do you know of our activities here of late?"

"What we've read in the papers..."

Sylvia nodded. "The papers cannot be bothered to print the truth since the truth will not sell papers. Get comfortable, and I will give you the facts. Although the communist ideals are alive and well, the party is facing a schism over how to achieve them. Some, like Ben Bradley and myself, favour a gradual progression. Others want to fight now to push out the government."

"Why don't you and Ben want to fight?" Dora asked.

"This country, and the world at large, has seen too much war. Too much loss. The people will not thank us for bringing death to their doorstep once again. Ben and I see the value of working with parties such as Labour because of the stability such an alliance provides."

"Is there a formal alliance?" Inga asked.

"The Tories would have us believe so, but I am not so foolish as to take their claims at face value." Sylvia's cheeks flushed. "Labour used to be more welcoming. Now that they have power, they are closing ranks against outsiders."

Sylvia's answer suggested she was not aware of the conversations between McAlister and Bradley. Dora pried deeper to make sure. "Would you consider abandoning the communist name and joining Labour? What of Ben Bradley?"

"I have won many badges in my days, but to answer your question, no, I would not. I must fight for my beliefs, even if it costs me. Ben is different. He values the spirit over the name. If Labour committed to doing all it could for the working man, then he might consider operating under their auspices." Sylvia thought for a moment and then added, "Do not mistake that for weakness. Ben has kept a disparate bunch in line for years. The only reason he has an open mind is because Trotsky himself gave him permission."

Dora filed that information away. "You have provided us the background. Now I would like to learn what you think of Ben Bradley as a person. Do you consider him a friend? Would you trust him in a business deal?"

"I consider you a friend, Theodora, for we are of like minds on many fronts. Ben is a colleague. He keeps me close because of the reputation of me and my family. If I left the party today and moved on to another cause, we would likely lose touch. For that reason, I would not sign on to a permanent business alliance. But if he asked me to be an early investor in something, I would say yes."

Dora moved the conversation on to other matters, asking about Sylvia's plans for the year and sharing tidbits of gossip she thought the woman would appreciate. An hour later, she and Inga took their leave. Before she left, she asked Sylvia to do her the small favour of vouching for her if Ben asked.

"I will do you one better—I am meeting him for lunch. Perhaps I will mention that my old friend, Theodora Laurent, stopped by to visit."

* * *

After lunch at home, Dora slid into the car next to Clark. He stared morosely straight ahead. Dora elbowed him to get his attention. "Don't you dare count yourself out before the game has properly begun, Clark Kenworthy. If there was ever a man who pulled victory from the ashes, it is you." Dora reached over and lifted the ends of his moustache up where they would be if he would only smile. "Now tilt that mouth of yours upwards to match and you will find your confidence follows behind. I promise."

She gave him such a stern look that he could not help but laugh. "Has there ever been a man you failed to charm?"

"At first, sure. But they all wear down, eventually. I decided a helping hand would not be remiss. While you and Rex were out, I paved my way into earning Ben Bradley's confidence, so you need not worry about that."

Ben Bradley's factory was situated in the bustling East End of London, a district teeming with industrial activity. The large, red-brick building was a hub of activity, with the rhythmic clatter of machinery audible from the outside. Clark explained Bradley was well-regarded for his commitment to the welfare of his workers, advocating for fair wages and safe working conditions, embodying his dedication to communist principles.

They found Ben in his office, waiting for them. The red rims around his eyes suggested he had already heard the news of Leonard's death. Dora offered Ben her deepest condolences after they were comfortable in his office.

"It is a terrible loss," he said in a hoarse voice. "I plan to visit

33

his family, but I stuck around to speak with you first. Please don't take this as an insult, Miss Laurent, but I was unaware you shared our ideals until I spoke with Sylvia Pankhurst."

"The Great War dispelled any notion I had of there being only one right way. It is more accurate to say I keep an open mind than to claim allegiance to any single party."

"That is why I asked Miss Laurent to help with the current matter. We have reason to believe that Leonard might have been the true target."

"What?" Ben rocked sideways and then gripped onto his armrests. "But I heard it was a letter addressed to McAlister. A matter of poor luck."

"We kept some information from the police," Clark explained while still omitting the key details. "I do not need to explain the need for absolute discretion. Miss Laurent keeps any number of secrets and has experience in handling tricky situations."

Dora did not want to leave the other man overlong to consider Clark's explanation. She leapt in with her first question. "Would you mind telling me about Leonard? If it isn't too painful, that is."

"It feels good to speak of him. Where would you like me to begin?"

"How did he come to your attention?"

Ben shifted to sit more comfortably. "Leonard joined the party during university, which is not uncommon. What set him apart was his thoughtful manner."

"What do you mean?" Dora asked.

"The younger members tend to be more emotional. They are filled with the fires of injustice, like cannons lining a field. You have but to point them in a direction. Their fuses are always lit. It is my job to pull them back and to teach them the benefits of thinking first."

"Leonard was not like that," Clark said, speaking up. "I noticed that about him in meetings in Parliament. I never caught him daydreaming, nor showing any emotion. He took in every word, listened to every opinion."

"That was why I picked him for the task," Ben explained. "His peers respected his words because he did not share them often. Of all our young people, I believed him the best hope for bringing back a balanced view on the possibility of working within the Labour party."

That made his death that much more of a loss. Dora added this to what she had already learned. A picture was emerging, but whether it was accurate remained to be seen.

"How did Leonard feel about his assignment? I imagine it put him at odds with some of his peers who did not take kindly to his apparent defection."

"Some were curious, which was exactly as I hoped. Others wrote him off as a lost cause. It happens. Being a communist is viewed negatively in most social circles. Some of the men have lost their jobs because of their association with us. I hire as many of them as I can, but I do not have space for them all." Ben scrubbed his face and drew a ragged breath.

Clark gave a subtle nod toward the door. Dora was not quite done yet.

"Mr Bradley, I realise this is unpleasant to contemplate, but can you think of anyone within your group who might have wished him harm?"

"I cannot think of anyone who hated him enough to kill him. However, sooner or later, you will come across this man's name. I'd rather you hear the full story from me."

Clark and Dora leaned forward. Ben Bradley had their full attention.

"Leonard's closest mate took the defection hard. The two

had words one night. Nearly came to blows from what I heard. But his is the last name I would put on your list."

"Give it to us, nonetheless. With luck, we can quickly rule him out," Dora said.

The communist leader took a piece of paper and scribbled down some notes. "I also included the name of Leonard's lady friend. She may know something useful."

Chapter 6
Good Cop, Bad Cop

Rex opened the front door and welcomed Clark and Dora inside. Dora's eyes sparkled with possibilities. Clark wore the dull-eyed, far-off stare of a man walking in his sleep.

Rex ushered them into the rear sitting room and insisted Clark avail himself of the sofa. "Stretch your legs out, man, and rest before you fall over."

"I don't understand why I am so exhausted. This is far from the first time I have stayed up past dawn."

Dora offered him a knitted throw. "It is the emotional toll compounding things. You've handled all the urgent tasks. Lie here for a little while and let us do some of the work."

Clark wanted to argue, but when he opened his mouth, a gigantic yawn escaped. "Very well, I will do as Miss Laurent orders. But you must promise to wake me should anything urgent arise." Rex and Dora pledged to do as requested. They made sure he was comfortable and then slipped from the room. They found the housemaid, Cynthia, dusting outside and asked her to ensure Clark was not disturbed.

"Harris is waiting in the drawing room," Rex explained. "He will be eager to hear what you learned." Indeed, Harris was all business. He had his pad of paper and pencil ready to take notes. "What did you think of Ben Bradley?" he asked once they were all seated.

"The best way I can find to describe him is as a grounded idealist."

Harris wrinkled his nose. "That is an oxymoron if I've ever heard one."

"Then allow me to expand on my description. He is a firm believer in communist ideals, but he knows that saying such things out loud has repercussions."

Rex contemplated Dora's answer. It certainly was not what he expected her to say, although it made sense. If Ben Bradley were a fiery revolutionist, he hardly would have entered an alliance with Clark and McAlister.

"What of him as a potential suspect?" Rex asked.

Dora gave a firm shake of her head. "The man was devastated, and I am experienced enough to tell the difference between guilt and sadness. Ben Bradley is firmly in the second camp."

Rex studied his wife. "You have far too satisfied a look on your face to have come away empty-handed."

"Who said anything about being empty-handed?" Dora opened her small clutch and pulled a piece of paper out. "I present to you the name and contact information for Leonard's volatile best friend and his girlfriend." Rex took the paper from his wife's outstretched hand. He glanced over the information but recognised neither name. He passed it on to Harris while Dora told them of the blow-up between the friends.

"Walter Philipson," Harris read out. "His name does not ring any bells. When will you go see him?"

"It is not a question of when, but how. I cannot imagine this Walter to be the type to welcome Lord Rex and his gossip-column girlfriend into his home." Dora shrugged her shoulders. "Any suggestions?"

Rex had a stash of clothing he kept for occasions. Which combination would serve him best was the question? Could he and Dora pretend to be fellow communists? If so, how should they look? He doubted they wore the dark suits of the Westminster clerks.

"I've got one," Harris said, intruding into Rex's deep thoughts. "How about sending the police to speak with him?"

"How would we explain that?"

"Not the real police. I still have several of my suits from my old days as a detective. Don't you have a uniform?"

"The one I wore to that fancy dress party?" Rex pulled a face. "No one will believe I am a real officer."

"Now darling," Dora said, cutting in. "You know as well as I do that the disguise is the least important part. With the right attitude and comportment, you can play most anyone convincingly."

"She is right," Harris chimed in. "Let me do most of the talking and you will be fine." Harris sat forward and rubbed his hands together. "I will be the grumpy, jaded old detective. You can be the trainee who still believes in the goodness of man. If I don't break him, you can try to coax the truth from him."

"That is all well and good, but you are still overlooking a flaw in your plan. What happens when the Met shows up for real? Or what if they have already sent someone to interview this man?"

Dora wagged a finger at her husband. "The Met thinks McAlister was the target. They have no reason to speak with anyone connected to Leonard."

Rex knew when he was beaten. He threw his hands in the air and said he would go change. Twenty minutes later, he met

Harris at the rear of the house. Harris was accompanied by Inga, who wore a coat and carried her handbag.

"Are you joining us?" Rex asked.

"No, I need to stretch my legs. I'll leave the costume fun to the pair of you." With a wave of her hand, she left the men studying one another.

There was no sign of Harris's normally affable personality. Gone too were the man's brightly coloured ties. Instead, he wore a dark suit made of cheap wool, with shiny patches on the knees and elbows testifying to the years of use.

It wasn't just the clothes, however. Harris glowered at Rex as he huffed at him to hurry. "You should have already had the car running, boy."

Rex caught on quickly. "Sorry, sir. I had forgotten my notepad. It won't happen again."

Harris winked at Rex. "You'll do. We'll take the Model T. For once, you can drive."

Getting comfortable behind the wheel was easier said than done. The uniform pinched and itched in equal measure. For one accustomed to tailor-made suits of the finest cut, Rex gained a newfound appreciation for what he had. The upside was that the ill-fitting uniform would act as a permanent reminder to stay in character.

Walter Philipson's address was in a rough section of Whitechapel, where narrow, cobblestone streets twisted between tightly packed rows of soot-stained buildings. The air was thick with the smell of coal smoke and the distant clanging of machinery from nearby factories.

Rex located a parking space near Philipson's boarding house. He climbed out of the car and scanned his surroundings. Curtains on the houses across the street twitched as the occupants peered out. Further ahead, a passing man caught sight of Rex's uniform and turned to go back the way he came.

Rex wondered for a moment about why that man might avoid the police before remembering the purpose of his visit.

Rex adjusted his cap and headed to the front doorstep. A dour-faced older woman answered. She wiped her flour-covered hands on her apron before addressing them.

"Can I help you, officers?"

"Afternoon, ma'am." Rex softened his accent to make it less upper crust and more working man. "Is Walter Philipson a resident here?"

"He is. I don't want any trouble."

"Nor do we," Harris said from where he stood on Rex's right. "We just need to have a word with him. Is he in?"

"Happens that he is. Came home early claiming to have taken ill. Let me see if he is capable of coming down. You can wait in the parlour."

The room was small and cold, the morning fire having burnt out. A threadbare throw failed to hide the aging sofa, but there was not a speck of dust to be seen. The owner took pride in her home, even if she did not have the funds to repair it.

A shadow in the doorway heralded Philipson's arrival. He stopped on the threshold and gave Rex and Harris a wary look. "Mrs Potts said you wanted to speak with me."

"We do. Take a seat." Harris stepped aside to give Philipson the first choice of seating. The young man chose the armchair, likely thinking it would leave him sitting higher than the others.

Harris chose the sofa opposite. He leaned back and stretched his legs wide, giving every appearance of a king on a throne. Rex remained standing, taking up position near the door. Philipson shifted uncomfortably, as though realising he had made a mistake.

Rex and Harris had decided on the drive over to keep their initial questions vague.

Harris spoke in a deep, gruff voice. "Walter Philipson?"

41

After the younger man nodded, he continued, "Your name has come up in a recent investigation."

Philipson tried to play it cool, but a tremor in his hand gave him away. "Oh?"

"We understand you are a close friend of Leonard Thompson. Or you were a close friend," Harris said.

"Is that why you are here?"

"It is one of the reasons," Harris answered. "Where were you yesterday?"

"Not at Westminster," Philipson said with a scowl. "Before you ask, word of Leonard's death spread like wildfire through the factory. Now you're here. You think the heavies at Westminster gate would let someone like me inside? You ask me, even if Leonard's fancy politician came down himself, the guards would still ban me."

"Is there a specific reason for that?"

Philipson pulled back and wrinkled his brow. "I'm a card-carrying communist, or I would be if such cards existed. They have photographed me at a few rallies. I am sure they keep tabs on such things."

Rex agreed, but that did not stop him from making a different point. "They let Leonard inside just fine. What makes you different from him?"

Philipson's expression darkened. "Unlike some, I stick to my convictions. Leonard used to feel the same until he let a skirt distract him. He tossed his ideals by the wayside and joined forces with the enemy."

"According to the Tories, the Labour party is a close friend of the commies," Harris growled.

"The only friends we have are the men and women who survive on the same breadcrumbs as we do. No one who sits at the table of power is truly on our side." Philipson closed his hands into fists. "I heard it was poison, meant for the House

42

leader. Leonard supped at the power table. That's why he is dead."

"Supped?" Rex tilted his head in confusion.

"Yeah—he must have eaten or drunk something meant for his boss. Or for all I know, maybe his duties included being a food taster. Either way, good luck tying this crime to me. I have honest work for honest pay, and it doesn't have anything to do with parliament or any of them lords and ladies there."

Philipson's smirk was so full of confidence, Rex believed he spoke the truth. The young man truly did not know how his friend had died. If he was lying to cover his tracks, he had missed his calling for the stage.

There would be nothing to gain from lingering. Rex cast Harris a surreptitious glance. His partner flipped his notebook closed and tucked it away.

"Don't leave town until we give you permission," Harris said.

Philipson rolled his eyes. "Sure, mate, although this will mess with my plans for a weekend country house party."

"Save the sarcasm for the broadsheets, son." That said, Harris stood and marched out of the room.

Rex followed behind, but he gave Walter Philipson one last look. The confident expression was gone. In its place was a solemnity that spoke of mourning. There was something else there, too. It hovered in his eyes as they flicked left and right.

Rex would have bet money that something else was fear. But of what? Discovery? Or fear for his life?

Chapter 7
Inga Wins the Day

Inga returned home less than an hour later. She swanned into the drawing room with a very satisfied expression on her face and availed herself of her favourite armchair.

"I would offer you a cup of tea, but you have the same look on your face as Mews does after Cook gives him a bowl of cream. You have only to swipe a paw over your mouth, and the resemblance would be complete," Dora said.

"Don't mind me. I'm simply enjoying a rare moment of being a full step ahead of Theodora Laurent."

"Oh?" Dora arched a carefully plucked eyebrow. "There is no need to let the suspense build. Do tell."

Inga required no further prodding. She leaned forward and did as Dora said. "Leonard's girlfriend. Harris told me her name before he and Rex left. There was something about it that rang familiar, but I couldn't put my finger on it."

"So you went to see someone? To the library?"

Inga shook her head, sending her auburn hair swinging. "I went for a walk. You know how good fresh air is for the mind. I was two streets over when I remembered."

Dora narrowed her gaze. "You mean to say that is when you

44

saw something that jogged your memory? Do not deny it. If whatever it was had been that close to the surface, you would not have needed to take a walk."

Inga huffed in annoyance. "Would it kill you to just once let me have a win?"

Dora tossed her head back and laughed. "The win is all yours, my dear. I am simply establishing the parameters of the prize. Now enough stalling. Why was her name familiar?"

"Shoe polish."

"Shoe polish?" That certainly was not what Dora expected Inga to say. Despite her impressive intellect, she could not make any sense of Inga's answer.

"Rex's valet mentioned he had found a new shoe polish that worked wonders. He asked me to pass along the recommendation to Harris, but I forgot."

"I am still failing to follow your logic here."

"It was Thornberry polish. Anita Thornberry's family manufactures it. With that information in hand, I did some research into the family. Mr Thornberry is an ardent, and generous, supporter of the Labour Party. They don't just make shoe polish—they have a whole line of leather care products, and they also manufacture high-quality footwear and fashion accessories. Their diversification into household cleaning products has also significantly boosted their wealth."

"Oh, that is useful," Dora exclaimed. "Now it makes sense why a communist would consider switching sides."

"Love woos us into all kinds of strange situations, as you and I both know well. Does this move the young Miss Thornberry up or down your suspect list?"

Dora crossed her arms and considered the question. "That all depends on how much Anita knew of Leonard's changing allegiance. And we won't know that until we speak with her."

"How do you want to handle the approach? Shall we wake

Clark? Cynthia caught me when I came in and said he was asleep in the sitting room."

Dora took her time in coming up with an answer. She was as loath to wake Clark as she was to exclude him. She focused her mind first on what advantages he might bring. Other than a familiarity with Leonard, she could not find any. It was not as though they could offer much of an explanation for Clark's and Leonard's connection. There was little reason a member of the House of Lords should be chummy with a lowly clerk.

So who would send a pair of women over to speak with Miss Thornberry? The police were out of the question. Even if Dora could find a shared friend to introduce them, that would not explain her interest in the young woman's dead beau.

A party? No, she corrected herself. The party. The Labour Party might send someone to check on the girl, especially given the importance of her father.

Dora blinked a few times to bring herself back to the present and then turned to Inga. "We are going to need to change our clothes."

"Oh no," Inga grumbled, though she put little heart in it. "Please tell me we don't have to dress as maids. Or men."

"Nothing of the sort. In fact, what you have on now might work if you swap your jumper and shoes for something less expensive."

Inga glanced down at her favourite wool jumper, one with a criss-cross pattern decorating the neckline, hem, and cuffs. "How can my jumper be a problem?"

"Because it was custom made in Paris. We need good British clothing if we are going to pass as representatives of the Labour Party."

A wide smile spread across Inga's face. "Finally, a role I can embody without too much effort."

Dora had to dig a little deeper into her extensive wardrobe

to find something appropriate. In the end, she settled on a staid grey dress that hung straight down, disguising her figure.

Rex shivered in horror whenever she pulled it out, but even he had to admit, it served its purpose.

Next, Dora used her cosmetics to add fine lines around her eyes and mouth, and shadows beneath her eyes. She pinned her strawberry blonde curls up and pulled a chestnut wig into place. Cynthia helped her style the wig into a simple twist favoured by older women.

Not to be outdone, Inga had used a bit of powder to add some white strands to her hair. She, too, had emphasised the tiny crow's feet beside her eyes.

Handbags at their sides, they left for the underground. They had their cover story in place by the time they arrived. Fortunately, they had rung in advance, learning that Miss Thornberry did not reside in the family residence. Instead, she had a room in a respectable boarding house close to Leonard's address.

"I find myself liking Miss Thornberry," Dora commented as they walked along the pavement.

"You have not even met her yet," Inga pointed out.

"Any young woman who dares to flee the nest without going straight into matrimony gets a point in favour in my book."

"Fair enough. I, however, am going to withhold judgment. One of us needs some semblance of impartiality."

Anita Thornberry's boarding house was in the elegant district of Chelsea. The area was a favourite among writers, artists, and intellectuals, contributing to its lively and cultured atmosphere. As Dora and Inga walked along the pavement, they admired the well-kept townhouses and quaint shops that lined the streets.

It was a world away from Leonard's residence in Battersea, just across the river with its industrial landscape and rows of modest terraced houses. Despite the proximity of the two neighbourhoods, they were worlds apart.

The boarding house itself, a handsome building with a pristine exterior and neatly trimmed hedges, fit seamlessly into Chelsea's upscale environment. Large bay windows allowed sunlight to stream into the elegantly furnished rooms. It exuded a certain charm and welcoming feel. Without hesitation, Inga walked to the front door and rang the bell.

After a minute's wait, an older woman answered. She eyed them both with piqued curiosity. She was a petite woman with a slight stoop, her grey hair neatly pinned back in a bun. Her sharp brown eyes missed nothing as she studied Dora and Inga from head to toe. "Can I help you?"

Dora kept a tight hold on her expression. A nosy landlady was the bane of a lodger's life, but she suited Dora's purpose. If Anita Thornberry was not forthcoming, a conversation with the landlady would fill the gaps. "Good afternoon," Dora said in a pleasant tone. "We are here to see Miss Thornberry. Is she home?"

The woman's expression dimmed. "I am afraid she is out."

"Do you expect her back soon?"

"Yes," the woman said without glancing at her watch. "She was off to do some shopping and then having lunch with a friend. At Claridge's," she added in an awed tone.

Dora and Inga looked suitably impressed.

"I thought you might be her. She has had a couple of telephone calls, but the man refused to leave his name. Not very gentlemanly of him, if you ask me. The old manners seem to be lost on this generation," she said with a much-put-upon sigh. "But here I am nattering on while you two nice ladies stand on the doorstep. Please, come in. You can wait in the sitting room."

The house was spotless and perfectly in order. There were no signs of any difficulty with funds. The curtains boasted a bright, unfaded colour, and an exquisitely carved clock kept time on the mantle. Dora was so taken by it she moved closer to investigate.

"My husband restored them in his spare time. I always said he worked too hard, but he lacked the patience to sit and simply be. He died while gardening five years ago." Dora murmured a sympathetic word and then joined Inga on the sofa.

"I hope we are not keeping you from anything, Mrs..."

"Sampson. Not at all. I'm sorry, I did not catch your names."

"I am Mrs Laurence and this is Mrs Keble," Dora said.

"How do you know Anita?" the woman asked.

"Truth be told, we have not met her yet. But we have a shared acquaintance." Mrs Sampson opened her mouth to pose another question, but the creak of the front door opening and a woman's voice interrupted her. "It's only me, Mrs Sampson," the voice called from the corridor.

"That's Anita," the woman said in a hushed tone before raising her voice. "Anita, could you come in here? You have guests."

The young woman who came into the room was in her early twenties, with a fresh, youthful beauty that radiated confidence and charm. Her wavy chestnut hair framed a face with delicate features, bright hazel eyes, and a complexion that spoke of outdoor leisure and good health. Dressed in the latest fashion, she carried herself with a carefree grace, her every movement exuding the effortless poise of someone accustomed to privilege and comfort.

Anita showed no hint of sadness, leading Dora to believe the woman was still unaware of the events of the previous evening. This added a layer of difficulty to the situation, but Dora did not complain. Although she hated to break the news, she would at least bear witness to the woman's reaction. In situations such as this, that could be telling.

"Hello?" Anita phrased her greeting as a question.

"Anita, this is Mrs Laurence and Mrs Keble. They were just about to tell me how they came to visit you."

Annoyance flashed across Anita's face before she could school her expression.

"We are here on behalf of the party. I am sorry to say we bear sad news. Perhaps you would care to sit?" Dora said.

Anita left her shopping bags in the doorway and moved toward a wooden straight-back chair. She perched on the edge of it and clasped her hands together.

Dora softened her mouth and tone. "There is no easy way to say this. It is about your beau, Leonard Thompson." Anita's fingers turned white as she tightened her grip. "Late last night, he suffered a terrible incident at Westminster. By the time anyone found him, it was too late."

"He's dead?" The gasped words came from the landlady. When Inga gave a nod of confirmation, the woman released a wail. Dora had not shifted her gaze from Anita's face.

Anita remained eerily still, her face a mask of shock. The colour drained from her cheeks, leaving her complexion ashen. For a long moment, the only sound in the room was Mrs Sampson's muffled sobs.

Finally, Anita spoke, her voice barely above a whisper. "How... how did it happen?"

Dora leaned forward, her voice gentle. "The details are still unclear. The police are investigating. We came because we know how close you two were. Leonard spoke of you often. We wanted to convey our sympathy."

Anita's eyes darted between Dora and Inga, a flicker of suspicion crossing her features. She took a deep breath, seeming to steel herself. "I do not believe it was an accident. Leonard was... he was growing paranoid lately. He was certain he was being spied upon."

Mrs Sampson gasped, but Dora ignored her, focusing intently on Anita. "What made him think that?" she probed gently.

"He said he noticed people following him, that his desk at work had been disturbed." Anita's voice quavered. "I thought he was just overworked, imagining things. But now..."

Inga leaned in. "Did he mention any specific concerns? Any threats?"

Anita shook her head. "He was vague. Said it was better if I didn't know details. For my safety, he said." Her eyes welled with tears. "I should have taken him more seriously."

Dora reached out, patting Anita's hand. "You couldn't have known. Did Leonard mention any changes at work? New responsibilities, perhaps?"

"He was excited about some project, but wouldn't say what. Said it could change everything." Anita's voice broke. "I thought he meant for us, our future. But maybe..."

Mrs Sampson, who had been hovering anxiously, suddenly interjected. She rose from her seat and hurried to wrap an arm around Anita. "Oh, you poor dear. Let's get you upstairs and into bed." She turned back to glare at Inga and Dora on her way out of the room. "Our visiting hours are over. Please see yourselves out."

Chapter 8
A Second Nightmare

Clark awoke with a jolt to find a shadow looming over him and sharp teeth sinking into his shoulder. He flailed his arms in defence and the shadow shifted backwards, but another attacker lay draped across his legs.

"My Lord! Lord Clark!" the shadow cried in a surprisingly feminine voice. Clark blinked until his eyes opened enough to make sense of his surroundings. The woman shifted over slightly, but it was enough to allow the late afternoon sun coming through the window to illuminate her face.

It was Cynthia, Dora's housemaid. She wore a bemused smile on her face.

"My lord, you had a telephone call. It was his grace, and he was most insistent I wake you."

His grace? Clark hesitated a guess. "Lord Audley?"

Cynthia bobbed her head. "He asks that you come over straight away."

No one needed to explain why. The spy leader wanted to know why someone made an attempt on the life of the leader of the House of Lords. Given their last conversation, he was right to think Clark might have an explanation.

Somehow, Clark doubted the truth was going to make the man feel better. He pushed the blanket back and made to get up, eliciting a yowl of disagreement from the cat draped across his legs. He supposed he should have been grateful for the warmth, but the orange and white hairs clinging to his trousers were a high price to pay.

"I will get a clothing brush from upstairs," Cynthia said. "I put a tray on the side table should you wish to eat something before you leave."

Clark found a damp cloth to wash his face and hands, along with a pot of tea and a plate of sandwiches. He ate them out of necessity rather than any genuine desire. Girding his loins and all that. When the maid returned, he asked about the others.

"Lord Rex and Mr Harris left two hours ago dressed as police officers. Miss Laurent and Miss Kay left more recently and did not say when to expect them back."

So Clark was on his own. It was appropriate given he alone had got them into this.

When he was ready, he accepted Archie's offer to drive him. In the back seat of Rex's Rolls-Royce, he dragged the memories of his earlier activities to the forefront of his mind.

He and Dora had left Ben Bradley's office with two names. Clark made an educated guess that the 'police officers' had gone to see Leonard's old friend, leaving Dora and Inga to visit the girlfriend. Perhaps even now, Rex and Harris were on their way back with the villain.

Cheered by that thought, Clark thanked Archie for the ride and then rapped the heavy knocker on the front of Audley's Mayfair door. Remembering Dora's advice, he twisted the ends of his moustache and fixed a serious expression on his face.

Audley's butler showed him inside to Lord Audley's study. The message was implicit. This was not a social call to be done in the drawing room over tea and cakes. The butler did not even ask Clark if he would like a drink before he left the men alone.

Lord Audley sat behind his ornately carved desk and peered at Clark with the unmoving stare of a head teacher.

"Do we have a problem?" Audley asked.

The question left Clark at a loss for words. He supposed he should be grateful Audley considered the problem to be shared. But in his heart, Clark felt responsible for bringing on all of this trouble.

Still, Lord Audley had not trained him to fall on his sword at the first sign of trouble. Clark drew himself up and matched his mentor's dry tone.

"We may, though that remains to be seen, your grace. I have already engaged Rex and Dora in assisting with the matter. I was awaiting their return when you rang."

Audley's expression did not change, but he relented enough to offer Clark a chair. It was an un-cushioned wooden chair, but at that moment, softness would have been dangerous, anyway.

Clark did not have the same relationship with Lord Audley as Rex and Dora. They were the ones called to clean up a mess. Clark's role was to help them avoid it in the first place. From almost the start, Audley had insisted they speak to one another as equals.

If Clark would one day lead, he had to show evidence of that capacity from the beginning. He dared not apologise or show any other hint of an emotion beyond confidence. He coughed into his hand to clear the frog that seemed lodged in his throat.

"I discovered the clerk's body last night. The man was known to me, for reasons I will explain next. The circumstances of his death were..." Clark trailed off to search for the right word. "Were less than ideal. I rang Rex, and with his help, I was able to remove any, erm, eyebrow-raising evidence from the scene."

There, that was safe and accurate enough.

"You did not find a dead body in McAlister's office to be eyebrow-raising on its own? The only thing worse would be if it was McAlister dead instead of the clerk."

Was that worse? Clark was not sure. "You may feel differently when you hear the full story. Shall I go back and start from the beginning?" Clark waited for Audley to nod before continuing. "I came up with a way to neutralise the communist threat here in England. A possible way," he amended.

In an unflinching tone, Clark explained his rationale, described his early meetings with the leaders of the two sides, and how he had addressed their concerns.

Audley interjected every now and again, requesting specifics on discussions. He wanted to know how Leonard had been chosen and what vetting Clark had done before sending him into McAlister's employ. After that, Clark brought the man up to speed.

"Dora and I visited Ben Bradley this afternoon, and he gave us a name of a possible suspect. That is where Rex and Harris are now. With any luck, we will hear good news from them soon."

Audley's quirked eyebrow suggested nothing about this situation could be good news, but Clark kept a stiff upper lip.

"If the communists went after their own, there is nothing you could have done to stop them," Audley said after a long pause. "Let us discuss what to do next."

They did not get far in their discussions before the butler knocked on the study door.

"The Dowager Duchess rang and has asked you both to attend her at your earliest convenience."

Rex's grandmother's home was a favourite neutral ground

the team used for their secret meetings with Lord Audley. Clark welcomed the respite as he pulled on his coat. He regained his good humour as the two men crossed Grosvenor Square to the Dowager Duchess's home on the other side.

After he and Lord Audley left their coats and hats with a waiting footman, they proceeded into the drawing room where the others were already located. Rex's grandmother welcomed them with all the social graces of a leading hostess of the ton. She flashed Clark a gentle smile of encouragement and invited them to have a seat.

Clark said hello to Dora and Rex, and then chose a small sofa across from them. It was only then that he noticed the woman standing near the window. Prudence Adams was as much a new recruit to the team as he was. On paper, they were a duo, leaning on one another for support as Dora and Rex did. Their opposite tendencies had got them off to a rocky start.

They were not as bad as Lord Audley and Dora's father, who would argue over the colour of the clouds in the sky. It was more accurate to say they had opposite ways to get things done. Where he went left, she veered right.

They had butted heads until Clark's father died. Prudence, orphaned during childhood, was the only one in their immediate circle to know what it was like to lose a parent. She became his port in the storm.

Late one night, after too much Scotch, he had made the drunken mistake of kissing her.

It would have been easier if she had pushed him away and slapped him across the face for being a cad.

But she had not. The kiss had deepened until a boom of thunder brought them both to their senses.

They had avoided being alone ever since. Clark had not wanted her to bear witness to his foolish mistake.

It seemed the dowager duchess had taken that choice out of his hands.

Lord Audley, ignorant of the history between the pair, told Prudence to take the seat beside Clark so that they might get on with the updates. Clark inched closer to the armrest on his side, leaving her with more than enough space. She mirrored his motions, resulting in a sizeable gap between the two and causing Dora to roll her eyes.

As far as the femme fatale was concerned, they should give in to their attraction and get it out of their system. The problem was that Clark feared it would cause the exact opposite result, and he was not ready to face that.

Now, at least, they had more pressing matters to discuss.

"Clark has told me what he knows," Lord Audley said, addressing his words to Dora and Rex. "I assume you have done the same for Lady Edith and Prudence. Shall we move to the results of your discussions with the communists?"

Dora glanced at Rex, and he waved at her to do the honours.

"Between the two of us, we spoke with Walter Philipson, Leonard's former friend, and Anita Thornberry, Leonard's girlfriend. Philipson had a possible motive, but no access. Anita was unaware of Leonard's death before I broke the news. The only useful information we got is that Leonard was concerned someone was spying on him."

Clark spluttered, "Spying on him? If that is the case, why didn't he come to me or McAlister?"

"Perhaps he did go to McAlister," Prudence said from Clark's side.

"I assure you he did not," Clark returned. "We already spoke to McAlister this morning, and he mentioned nothing of the sort. Given the circumstances, I cannot see any reason for him to keep something like that to himself."

Clark assumed that would be the end, but Prudence offered a rebuttal.

"There is a glaringly obvious reason, and if you will stop and think for a moment, I am certain you will arrive at it."

Clark forgot all his intentions to keep his distance. He twisted around, bumping his leg against hers, so he could stare at her. "You don't mean—"

"That the killer might be within the Labour Party. Yes, that is exactly what I am saying. We would be fools to ignore the possibility." Prudence crossed her arms over her chest and practically dared him to disagree.

"Prudence is right," Dora said, cutting in before the pair went any further. "Rex and I were discussing this on the ride over."

Rex picked up the thread. "The more I thought about last night, the stranger the scene became. Leonard opened the letter, thought nothing of the powder, and then went about his duties. If he had washed his hands, or alerted a passing guard, he might still be alive. The communists are risk-takers, but not fools. They would not risk that Leonard might die and leave such evidence behind."

Any hopes Clark held of wrapping this up quickly evaporated into the aether. It took all his strength not to shrink under Lord Audley's weighty stare.

Audley clasped his hands together and rested them on his stomach. "This situation is more complicated than we thought. We must put all considerations back on the table. Was Leonard the target or was the letter supposed to be opened by McAlister? Either way, is there a chance the sender is someone within Parliament?"

Lord Audley's tone grew ever more steely as he outlined the possibilities. In turn, Clark's resolve to hold firm sprung leaks.

In the end, it was Lady Edith, the dowager duchess and eldest in the room, who came to his aid.

"Henry," she said, addressing Lord Audley with his given name, "let the man be for a moment. The Met officers are already looking into the possibility that McAlister was the target. Clark has rightly told the team to explore the alternative. I am sure he will go speak with McAlister again, given what we now know. Isn't that right, Clark?"

Clark's thoughts were in such a jumble that he had not decided on a next step. Lady Edith's suggestion was eminently reasonable.

"Err, yes, that is exactly what I plan. Rex, would you care to join me?"

Rex agreed, giving Clark an excuse to leave immediately. Though no one voiced the words aloud, he could hear them anyway.

Clark Kenworthy, Earl Rivers, had blundered in his first efforts at statesmanship.

Chapter 9
A Visit to the Gentlemen's Club

The sun slipped below the horizon as the two men got into the car. Rex glanced over at his passenger, noting the morose frown marring Clark's usually amiable features. They could go straight to Westminster and catch McAlister on his way out, but Rex quickly abandoned that line of thinking. Clark practically reeked of defeat, and it would do them no good for McAlister to catch wind of it.

Instead, he pointed the Rolls toward their club. Clark was so deep in thought that he did not notice their destination until Rex pulled up at the kerb and waved the valet forward.

"I realise I was lost in a world of my own, but did I miss a conversation whereby we agreed to come here instead of finding McAlister?" Clark asked.

"It was your own distraction that caused me to change direction. You cannot walk into Parliament looking as though you lost a war. At minimum, it will lead to questions. At worst, it will cause McAlister to lose faith in your abilities. We will go inside, have a drink, and see if we can't raise your spirits." With that, Rex exited the car.

Clark followed, albeit at a slower pace. He joined Rex on

the pavement and gazed at the facade of their private club. It was an exclusive haven for the elite, known for its plush leather armchairs and an air thick with the scent of cigars and brandy. Today, however, it held less appeal to Clark. He glanced over at Rex and shrugged his shoulders. "I fear such a thing is not in the cards, but I can see there is no point in arguing with you."

"There is not, and I will explain why. It is not our task to wage battles, nor to bask in the glory of a win. We are the ones called in when hope would otherwise be lost. We have always snatched victory from the jaws of defeat, and this will not be the exception." Rex studied his friend's face. "Do you understand what I mean?"

Clark gave a solemn nod of agreement, though his mouth was still pinched together. "Thank you for the reminder, Rex. I will endeavour to keep this thought in the forefront of my mind. Now, let us go inside."

Both men ordered a pint of ale, wanting to wet their tongues while keeping their wits about them. They found a pair of high-backed leather wing chairs set near a secluded alcove, its shadowed corners and heavy drapes offering an intimate space where they could speak with little fear of being overheard.

Rex took a long sip, savouring the rich, malty sweetness of the amber ale with its hint of caramel and a slightly bitter finish that lingered on his palate.

For his part, Clark was staring into his still full glass. After a long moment, he lifted his head. "Perhaps we should be more forthcoming with Bradley. If we told him about the letter, he might be of a different mind with regard to who is responsible."

Rex blanched, and his drink sloshed in his hand. "You cannot tell him! If he is behind this, we would lose what little advantage we have."

"Were you not the one suggesting a mere hour ago that guilt lay elsewhere?"

Clark's question gave Rex pause, but not for long. Rex answered, "Either way, we dare not trust the commies any more than is absolutely necessary. They rejoice in causing chaos."

Clark grimaced, but he did not raise further argument. He set his pint glass on the side table. "We should go. I find I have no taste for drink."

"It seems fate wants you to drink it anyway, for McAlister has just walked through the doorway." Rex raised his hand and waved to get the man's attention.

McAlister changed his path to come over to them rather than going to the bar. As soon as he was within earshot, he asked, "Have you any news?"

"Some," Rex replied, keeping his response suitably vague. "Get a drink while I see if there is a private room we can use."

The club butler located a small sitting room on the second floor. The room was richly furnished with dark wood panelling, an ornate fireplace, and deep, plush armchairs. McAlister dropped into a padded leather wingback, leaned back, and released a heavy sigh. Rex's stomach turned at the sight, knowing he was about to make things worse for the already exhausted man. Clark hid his grimace behind his pint of ale.

McAlister sat up straight and indulged in a gulp of his ale. "Gentlemen, I trust you will forgive me for the lapse in manners. It has been a day unlike any other in my life, and I desperately hope it will remain unique. Death cannot be avoided, but surely he can steer clear of my office for a long while."

Rex raised his glass in toast to McAlister's words, but when he took a drink, he choked trying to get it down. Clark slapped him on the back until he could breathe again.

McAlister looked upon Rex not with sympathy but concern. "You bring bad news. It is written in the lines on your face."

"We bring questions," Clark corrected while Rex wiped his

mouth, proving Rex's spluttering had an upside. As with all moments of difficulty, Clark pulled himself together and faced them head on.

"Before I answer anything, I would like to know what you learned from Bradley."

"Not much of use. Bradley is in a similar state to yourself. He is devastated by the loss of a promising young man and guilt-wracked at his own culpability," Clark said.

"So he admits he is to blame?" McAlister asked incredulously.

"He did not send the letter, if that is what you mean. I took an expert in body language with me. They could find no sign of a lie." Clark softened his voice. "He shares blame with me and with you. The three of us put Leonard in that room. We will spend the rest of our lives second-guessing that decision."

McAlister blinked a few times and then cleared his throat. "Let us put our energy toward identifying the culprit, so we might at least have closure."

"To do that, we must now ask you for information," Rex replied.

"Very well. I will do my best to answer anything you ask."

The men all set their drinks aside and got down to business. Clark began. "We are still exploring the possibility that the killer lies within the Communist Party. However, as part of our conversations with people close to Leonard, we discovered he had some concerns in recent days. Did he raise anything with you?"

McAlister was mystified. "Not at all."

"Did he act strangely? Was it normal for him to work so late?"

McAlister paused, his brow furrowing as he considered Clark's question. "Leonard worked hard. He was often the last to leave, not because I gave him so much to do, but because he volunteered for extra tasks." McAlister's eyes took on a distant look, as if he were seeing the young man in his mind's eye. "He was ambitious, that one. Always looking for ways to prove himself."

Rex leaned forward, his elbows resting on his knees. "Did you notice any change in his behaviour recently? Anything out of the ordinary?"

McAlister shook his head slowly. "Not that I can recall. He was his usual diligent self. Although..." He trailed off, his gaze fixed on some point beyond the richly panelled walls of the room.

"Although?" Clark prompted gently.

McAlister sighed, running a hand through his thinning hair. "It's probably nothing, but now that you mention it, there was one incident last week. I caught him looking rather worried when he thought no one was watching. When I asked if everything was alright, he brushed it off, saying he was just tired from burning the midnight oil."

Rex and Clark exchanged a glance.

"Did you believe him?" Rex asked.

"At the time, yes. Leonard wasn't one to complain, you see. Always had a stiff upper lip, that lad. But now, considering... recent events, I can't help but wonder if there was more to it."

Clark nodded thoughtfully. "It's possible he was dealing with something he didn't feel comfortable sharing. Did he have any close friends or confidants among the staff?"

McAlister shook his head. "Not that I'm aware of. He was friendly enough with everyone, but he kept to himself, mostly. Professional to a fault, that one."

Rex drummed his fingers on the arm of his chair. "What about outside of work? Did he ever mention any friends or acquaintances?"

"I'm afraid I didn't pry into his personal life," McAlister

admitted. "But now that you mention it, there is something else that might be relevant." He paused, taking a sip of his ale before continuing. "It's not about Leonard specifically, but it might shed some light on the situation."

Clark and Rex leaned in, their interest piqued. "Go on," Clark encouraged.

McAlister's voice lowered, as if he were sharing a secret. "There have been... rumblings of dissent within the party. Nothing overt, mind you, but whispers and sidelong glances. It started when I hired Leonard."

Rex's eyebrows shot up. "Because he was from outside the Labour Party?"

McAlister nodded grimly. "Precisely. Some felt I should have chosen someone from within our ranks. They saw it as a betrayal of sorts, bringing in an outsider for such a sensitive position."

Clark frowned. "Did anyone confront you about this directly?"

"No, no one had the gall to say it to my face," McAlister said, a hint of bitterness creeping into his voice. "But I'm not deaf to the gossip that floats around the corridors of power. There were mutterings about 'maintaining party loyalty' and 'protecting our interests.' All rot, if you ask me. I had my reasons for hiring Leonard, as you well know, and I know of no reason anyone should doubt my rationale, even if I did not share it."

Rex nodded slowly, processing this new information. "Do you have any idea who might have been behind these... rumblings?"

McAlister shook his head. "I'm afraid not. As I said, it was all very hush-hush. No one wanted to be seen as openly challenging my decision."

Clark leaned back in his chair, his face thoughtful. "It's

interesting that no one confronted you directly. That suggests a certain level of... what? Fear? Respect?"

"Both, I'd wager," McAlister replied. "The Labour Party is still finding its footing. We're a coalition of diverse interests, and maintaining unity is crucial. An open challenge to leadership decisions could be seen as divisive."

Rex nodded. "And in politics, the appearance of unity is often as important as unity itself."

"Precisely," McAlister agreed. "But make no mistake, gentlemen. While I may not have names, I'm certain there are those within the party who were less than pleased with Leonard's appointment."

Clark exchanged a glance with Rex before turning back to McAlister. "This is valuable information, sir. It opens up new avenues of investigation we hadn't considered before. We'll need to tread carefully. Any misstep could have far-reaching consequences beyond just solving Leonard's murder."

"Indeed," McAlister agreed. "Which is why I'm grateful for your discretion in this matter. The last thing we need is a scandal that could destabilise the party further."

Clark cleared his throat. "Given what you've told us, sir, we'll need to speak with more people within the party. Is there anyone you'd recommend we start with?"

McAlister thought for a moment, then his face brightened slightly. "As a matter of fact, there is someone who might be able to help. Ellen Liddell."

Rex raised an eyebrow. "I'm not familiar with the name."

"She's not an MP or an official party member," McAlister explained. "But she's a key volunteer within the Labour party. Ellen works closely with our newer, younger members, helping them get settled in London and involved in the social scene."

Clark nodded approvingly. "That sounds like exactly the

sort of person we need to speak with. Someone with their ear to the ground, so to speak."

"Precisely," McAlister agreed. "Ellen has a way of... knowing things. She's discreet, but she hears all sorts of gossip and chatter. If anyone can give you insight into the mood among the younger set, it's her."

Rex leaned forward. "And you think she might have heard something about the dissatisfaction regarding Leonard's appointment?"

McAlister nodded. "It's quite possible. Ellen has a talent for getting people to open up to her. She might have picked up on things that others missed."

Clark turned to Rex. "It sounds like Mrs Liddell should be our next port of call. Do you agree?"

Rex nodded decisively. "Absolutely. We need to piece together the mood within the party to see if we can identify any potential threats."

McAlister reached into his jacket pocket and pulled out a small notebook. He scribbled something on a page, tore it out, and handed it to Rex. "Here's Ellen's contact information. She's usually at party headquarters during the day, but you can also reach her at home in the evenings."

Rex pocketed the paper with a nod of thanks. "We appreciate this, sir. Please, do us the favour of not mentioning anything about our plans to speak with her. I've found a more informal approach often works better at extracting information."

McAlister bit back the questions on his tongue. "I will not question your methods, so long as they work. I just want to see justice done for Leonard. He was a good lad, and he deserved better than this."

Rex stood, straightening his jacket. "We'll do everything in our power to uncover the truth, sir. You have our word on that."

As they prepared to leave, McAlister called out, "One more

thing, gentlemen." They turned back to face him. "Please... be careful. If there are forces within the party working against us, they may not take kindly to your investigation."

Clark nodded solemnly. "We understand the risks. We'll proceed with the utmost caution."

With final handshakes exchanged, Rex and Clark left the private room, their minds buzzing with new information and possibilities. As they stepped out into the cool London evening, both men felt the weight of their task settling heavily upon their shoulders. With Ellen Liddell's contact information burning a hole in Rex's pocket, they set off into the night, determined to uncover the truth, no matter where it might lead them.

Chapter 10
The Makeover

Over dinner, Rex and Clark shared what they had learned with Dora, Inga, Harris, and Prudence. Clark suggested they ring Mrs Liddell straightaway, but Dora told him to keep his seat.

"Contacting Ellen Liddell will have to wait until the next morning, for reasons both practical and important," she said in a steady tone that brooked no arguments. "If we ring now with questions out of the blue, she is only going to be suspicious. It would be far better to cross paths with her at the party headquarters. Additionally, we are all meant to go out tonight. I promised Kate Meyrick we would put in an appearance at the 43."

Clark dropped his fork on his plate with a clatter, sending drops of sticky toffee sauce flying through the air. "Oh no, not that! I can't possibly go out and enjoy myself after the day I've had."

Dora softened her voice. "Believe me when I say I understand. But that is exactly why you must come along. You are expected. If you don't turn up, people will ask questions. I am not saying that you must dance and drink into oblivion, but rubbing elbows with the other guests is to the benefit of us all. Plus, we will give dear Prudence here an excuse to mention us in the papers."

Prudence bobbed her head in agreement. "That's true. If the infamous Theodora and Rex remain home two nights in a row, that will be a headline in itself. Perhaps, however, I might offer some help. Would you like me to come along? No one expects me to take the dance floor. You can use my presence as an excuse to stay at the table."

Clark gaped. "You would do that? But you hate Club 43 so much that you decline every invitation to join us."

Prudence stiffened. "It is not that much of an imposition. There's no need to make a fuss over it. If you don't need my help, I'll happily stay in."

Dora intervened before the pair could tailspin into another of their disagreements. "It is a splendid suggestion, Prudence, and very kind of you to offer. I am sure I have a gown upstairs that will suit you. Inga, will you help with her hair?"

"Of course, I will," Inga replied before Prudence could say no. "That blue gown of yours should do for Prudence just fine. In fact, you should make a gift of it. It is far too conservative for you, anyway."

Prudence relaxed at Inga's comment. "That's too kind of you. I will try it on and we can make the final decision together."

Dora nodded, though she had no intention of allowing Prudence to decline the gown. It was far past time for Prudence and Clark to admit their interest in one another. Putting them side-by-side in a dark club, with Prudence in something other than her high-necked, unflattering frocks, was almost certain to catch Clark's eye.

After dinner, Clark went home to change into something appropriate for a night out. He promised to join them at the club before midnight. That did not stop Dora from issuing a threat to come collect him herself if he failed to show.

With Clark suitably forewarned, Dora turned her attention to Prudence. She led Prudence upstairs to her bedroom, with Inga following close behind.

Prudence balked at the doorway, overwhelmed by the combination of the luxurious carpet, sleek bedroom furniture, and modern art that reflected Dora's exuberant personality. Inga nudged her forward and guided her to the dressing table.

"Now, darling," Dora said, throwing open her wardrobe, "let's find that blue gown for you."

Prudence fidgeted nervously. "Remember, I prefer to keep things simple."

Inga placed a reassuring hand on Prudence's shoulder. "Look at me, Prudence. I have far different tastes from Dora, but that doesn't stop her from gifting me clothing I love. Have some faith. She'll respect your wishes, but trust me. A little glamour never hurt anyone."

Dora emerged triumphantly with a sapphire blue silk gown. Its cut was modest by Dora's standards, but still more daring than Prudence's usual attire. The dress featured a slightly lower neckline and a shape that accentuated the waist before flowing elegantly to the floor.

"This is perfect," Dora declared. "It'll bring out your eyes beautifully."

Prudence hesitated before taking the dress. "It's lovely, but isn't it a bit... much?"

Inga chuckled. "You write the social columns, dear Prudence. You know better than us that by standards of those who frequent the 43, this is positively demure."

With gentle encouragement, they helped Prudence into the gown. As Dora made some minor adjustments to the fit, Inga set about styling Prudence's hair.

"How about we try a soft wave?" Inga suggested, running her fingers through Prudence's locks. "It'll frame your face nicely without being too dramatic."

Prudence nodded, still looking uncertain. "As long as it's not too elaborate."

As Inga worked on her hair, Dora approached with a small makeup case. "Now, let's add just a touch of colour to those cheeks."

"Oh, I don't usually wear—" Prudence began.

"Just a hint," Dora assured her. "We want to enhance your natural beauty, not mask it."

With expert hands, Dora applied a light dusting of rouge to Prudence's cheeks and a subtle tint to her lips. She stepped back, admiring her handiwork.

"There," Dora said, satisfied. "Simple, yet stunning."

While Dora got dressed in a glittering ruby gown, Inga finished styling Prudence's hair in soft waves that cascaded over her shoulders. "Perfect. Now, shall we let you see?"

Prudence took a deep breath and turned to face the full-length mirror. Her eyes widened in surprise as she took in her reflection.

The blue gown hugged her figure in ways her usual dresses never did, accentuating curves she hadn't realised she possessed. The colour made her eyes pop, while the subtle makeup brought a warm glow to her features. Her hair, usually pulled back, now framed her face in soft, flattering waves.

"Is that... really me?" Prudence whispered, barely recognising herself.

Dora beamed. "It most certainly is, darling. You look absolutely ravishing."

Inga nodded in agreement. "You'll turn every head in Club 43 tonight."

"You flatter me. With Theodora Laurent at my side, I'll be

surprised if anyone notices me there." Prudence blushed, a smile tugging at her lips. "It's so different, but... I think I like it."

"You should," Dora said, placing a strand of pearls around Prudence's neck as a finishing touch. "You look like yourself, just... enhanced."

As Prudence continued to admire her reflection, a newfound confidence seemed to settle over her. She stood a little straighter, her chin lifting slightly.

"Thank you both," she said softly. "I have long preferred to steer clear of the limelight. You have made me see that I can shine in my own way."

Dora and Inga exchanged knowing glances. Their mission was accomplished. Prudence was ready to step out of her comfort zone, if only for one night.

"Well then," Dora said, clapping her hands together. "Shall we go show Rex and Harris what we've done?"

With a final nod of approval from Prudence, the three women made their way downstairs.

Dora led the way into the drawing room and was delighted by the admiring and astonished gazes of the waiting men. Their compliments soothed the last of Prudence's fears, and she wore a bright smile when Harris helped her into one of Dora's fur coats.

That smile faded when Rex's Rolls-Royce Silver Ghost approached the front of the jazz club. A line of people, all dressed in their finery, waited outside. Flashes of light signalled the presence of photographers. Prudence gripped the edge of her seat and refused to budge.

"I can't do this. Isn't there a rear exit we can use?"

Dora pried Prudence's fingers from the leather before she could damage Rex's car. "You can do this. You can and you will. First, because you are far braver than you give yourself credit. Second, because I will drag you out of this car if I must."

Prudence's head snapped up and she goggled at Dora's bald threat. Dora's amused grin coaxed a self-deprecating laugh from the timid woman. "I would not put it past you."

"I suggest you not find out. Now Rex and I will exit first and put on a show to attract everyone's attention. You can glide past us and go straight into the club. Will that do?"

Prudence took a deep breath and then agreed.

Dora stepped out of the car first, her ruby gown catching the light of the camera flashes. She twirled dramatically, causing the sequins to shimmer and dazzle. Rex followed, smoothly sliding his arm around Dora's waist. With practiced ease, they struck a series of poses, Dora laughing vivaciously and Rex flashing his most charming smile. The photographers clamoured for more from Miss Laurent and her beau Lord Rex.

When Dora spotted Prudence exiting the car, she pretended to stumble. Rex, attuned to his wife's movements, caught her in a theatrical dip. The crowd gasped and cheered, their attention fully captured by the spectacle. Dora gave a final wave and blew a kiss to the crowd before sauntering into the club.

Clark had beaten them there and was holding court in Dora's favourite corner booth. If Rex had shown appreciation for Prudence's new glamour, Clark was absolutely thunderstruck. It took two requests for him to understand that Dora wanted him to slide over and make room.

She slid in next to him and motioned for Prudence to take the other side. While Prudence was scooting around the cushioned leather seat, Dora leaned close to Clark and whispered, "Tell Prudence how lovely she looks and maybe she'll stop wearing those dire frocks we both hate."

Clark gulped. "That's a lovely gown, Prudence."

Dora dug her elbow into his side.

"Erp, I meant to say you are radiant this evening. Far too stunning to hide yourself away in this corner."

Prudence blushed prettily. "You are too kind, Clark. But here I will stay, if my presence is not too much of an imposition. I did promise to keep you company."

They were off to a good enough start for Dora to feel confident about leaving them on their own. She offered to accompany Rex to the bar to order a round of drinks and slipped into the crowd of club goers before anyone could disagree.

The bar was not far away, but between the smoke of the many cigarettes and the wail of the trumpet keeping the dancers on their feet, Dora had only a hazy view of the couple they had left behind. Like her, Rex was equally interested in keeping an eye on them.

From their vantage point at the bar, Dora and Rex observed the pair in the corner booth. At first, all seemed well. Prudence's cheeks were flushed with a becoming pink, and Clark leaned in attentively as she spoke, his eyes never leaving her face. Dora allowed herself a self-satisfied smile, certain her plan was unfolding splendidly.

However, as the minutes ticked by while Dora and Rex waited to be served, a subtle change came over the scene. Prudence's posture stiffened, and she shifted incrementally away from Clark. The warmth in her expression cooled, replaced by a familiar look of polite detachment. For his part, Clark's brow furrowed, and his shoulders hunched forward defensively. The easy rapport they had shared moments ago had vanished, replaced by the tense atmosphere that so often surrounded them.

Rex let out a frustrated sigh. "Blast it all," he muttered, running a hand through his perfectly coiffed hair. "I thought for certain this time... What do you suppose has gone wrong now?"

Dora's lips pressed into a thin line as she watched Clark's

expression darken further. "I haven't the foggiest," she admitted. "One would think that after all our efforts to shine Prudence up, Clark might finally see past his own nose. But it seems even in that stunning gown, our dear Prudence hasn't managed to break through his thick skull."

"Or Prudence herself is the problem child tonight. Perhaps we ought to intervene," Rex suggested, taking a step in their direction. But Dora placed a restraining hand on his arm.

"No, darling. We've done all we can for tonight. If they're to sort this out, they must do it on their own terms." She sighed, her earlier optimism deflating like a punctured balloon. "Come, let's mingle. We've a reputation to uphold, after all, and I shall not let their squabbling ruin our evening."

With a final glance at the now clearly quarrelling pair, Dora took Rex's arm and steered him towards the dance floor. As the jazz band struck up a lively Charleston, she resolved to push thoughts of matchmaking from her mind. For now, at least, she would focus on the case at hand and leave matters of the heart for another day.

Chapter 11
Let's Go Volunteering

There was no talk of Clark and Prudence at the breakfast table the next morning. Instead, Dora and Rex discussed how to approach the next stage of their investigation into Leonard's untimely demise.

Rex scraped the last of the eggs from his plate onto the remaining bite of toast and then popped them into his mouth. After a swig of coffee, he made his opinion known. "Why don't you and I go? It has been a while since we've gone undercover together."

"Darling, as fun as that sounds, I must decline. Inga and I already established identities as members of the Labour party. It is in all our best interests that we continue using them, especially should we cross paths with Anita again." Dora reached over and caressed Rex's hand. "Should Ellen point us in another direction, I will come straight home and let you take the lead on the next interview. Is that a fair trade?"

"I suppose…" Rex's tone suggested he was not yet fully on board with the plan.

Dora added, "In the meantime, why don't you give Clark a

ring and see how he is doing? You could bring up the subject of how lovely Prudence looked last night?"

Rex brightened. "I'll get Harris to accompany me to pay Clark a visit. We two married men can extol the virtues of wedded bliss. Perhaps that will encourage Clark to push past whatever is standing between him and finding happiness with Prudence. Or any woman, really. He has been on his own for far too long."

Once again, Dora and Inga donned their now-dubbed Labour party outfits and comfortable Mary Jane shoes. The party office in Pimlico was close enough to Dora's Belgravia townhouse for the women to walk. Dora kept Inga entertained with stories from the night before until the new home of the Labour party came into view.

The Labour party had chosen well for its London base, as the townhouse on Ecclestone Street was near enough to Parliament for people to go back and forth. Ironically, they had laid claim to a former home of Winston Churchill, a man who had served in both the Conservative and Liberal parties, but had steadfastly avoided membership with the Labour movement. For Dora and Inga, it was a reminder of how quickly the winds of change could blow through the country, turning opponents into bedfellows and back to opponents again.

They opened the front door to find a battered wooden desk with a well-dressed woman sitting behind it. She appeared to be in her late forties, with the longer hairstyle preferred by the previous generation. In another decade, she would be the very picture of an adoring grandmother. Now, the glasses perched on her nose and cameo pin at her throat merely made her look stuffy. Dora's opinion changed when the woman glanced up from her work and smiled in welcome.

"Good morning. How can I help you?" she asked.

Dora introduced herself and Inga, using the names they

had provided to Anita Thornberry. She explained their interest in volunteering, saying, "We met Lord McAlister at a fundraising event and he told us to come here. He recommended we speak with Mrs Ellen Liddell. I don't suppose she is in today."

The woman's face brightened. "I'm Ellen Liddell. Lord McAlister sent you? And he mentioned me by name? That is quite an honour. Please, follow me to somewhere more comfortable so we can get to know one another better."

She rose from her chair and stuck her head into the nearest room, asking someone to man the front desk. She then led them into a former parlour turned break room, with several seating areas filling the space and a round table with four chairs tucked away in the corner. A man occupied one of the chairs at the table. He lowered the paper he was reading when they came in, but returned to his reading when he realised they were no one important.

Mrs Liddell bade them to take a seat while she fetched three cups of tea. She returned with three serviceable, plain white cups, a tiny pitcher of milk and a bowl of sugar cubes. Once she had settled into her chair, cup of tea in hand, she opened the conversation. "Now then, what draws you ladies to the Labour Party?"

Inga, in her role as Mrs Kay, leaned forward slightly. "Well, you see, I grew up near Manchester, in a working-class family. My father worked in the cotton mills, and I remember vividly the hardships we faced."

"Oh, yes," Mrs Liddell nodded sympathetically. "The textile industry has had its share of struggles."

"Indeed," Inga continued. "I'll never forget the winter of 1912, when the men went on strike. The whole town seemed to hold its breath. It was then I realised how important it was for workers to have a voice."

Mrs Liddell's eyes lit up with interest. "That must have been quite an experience for a young girl."

"It was," Inga agreed. "But it wasn't until the war that I truly understood the power of collective action. I served as a nurse, you see."

"Did you now? That must have been trying."

Inga nodded solemnly. "It was. But it also showed me how people from all walks of life could come together for a common cause. After the war, I knew I wanted to be part of something that could make a real difference in people's lives."

Mrs Liddell set her teacup down, clearly impressed. "Well, Mrs Kay, your experiences certainly align with our party's values. And what about you, Mrs Lawrence?" she asked, turning to Dora.

Dora opened her mouth to respond, but Inga smoothly interjected, "Oh, I've been talking Mrs Lawrence's ear off about the importance of the labour movement. We both feel strongly that now is the time to get involved, to help shape the future of our country."

Mrs Liddell beamed. "Well, ladies, I must say, your enthusiasm is refreshing. As it happens, my primary responsibility is working with our up-and-coming members— those clerks and newly minted members of the Commons who might one day be a future Prime Minister. We organise social events and the like. Might that be of interest to you? I can always use extra pairs of hands."

Dora and Inga exchanged glances, both pleased with how easily Mrs Liddell had offered them a way to discuss their topic of choice. Inga gave a subtle nod of encouragement for Dora to speak on their behalf.

"We assumed we would fold pamphlets or prepare cups of tea, and here you are giving us the chance to do something even more important. Imagine meeting all those young men and women, watching them grow into leaders! We would be honoured, to say the least." Dora allowed her smile to droop a little. "Oh, you must have known the clerk who died in Lord McAlister's office. What was his name? Leopold?"

Mrs Liddell's shoulders sank. "Leonard. Leonard Thompson, and yes, I did. We all did, in fact. It is truly a great loss to the party, for Leonard showed much spirit. He was eager to take on responsibilities, large and small."

"Too eager, if you ask me," a male voice said.

Dora turned to see that the man at the table had folded his paper and set it aside.

Mrs Liddell shot the man a reproachful look. "Mr. Graves, please. This is hardly the time for such comments."

Mr. Graves shrugged, unapologetic. "I'm merely stating facts, Mrs Liddell. The ladies asked, after all."

Dora, sensing an opportunity, leaned forward. "Oh? Was there something unusual about Leonard's eagerness?"

Mrs Liddell sighed, clearly torn between loyalty to the deceased and the need for honesty. "Leonard was... exceptionally motivated. He was a recent convert to the party, and I suppose that is why he felt he had something to prove. For my part, I thought his commitment to be admirable. Undoubtedly, Lord McAlister felt the same, which is why he invited the young man to become his personal clerk."

"And that raised a few eyebrows, didn't it?" Mr. Graves interjected. "A newcomer, rising so quickly?"

"It was unusual," Mrs Liddell admitted reluctantly. "But it is not for us to question why someone joins the party, but to simply be grateful our numbers are growing. Plenty of party members welcomed him."

Mr. Graves snorted. "Don't forget those who openly voiced their concerns about the lad's intentions, Mrs Liddell. You can't deny there were whispers."

Inga, playing her role perfectly, gasped. "Whispers? Whatever do you mean?"

Mrs Liddell looked uncomfortable. "Well, in any organisation, there are bound to be... differences of opinion. Leonard was quite progressive in his views, which some found invigorating and others found... challenging."

"Challenging?" Mr. Graves laughed. "That's putting it mildly. Do you ladies remember the debate we had last month about the party's stance on nationalisation?"

Dora and Inga shook their heads, feigning ignorance.

Mr. Graves leaned back in his chair. "Well, let me tell you. Young Leonard stood up and accused John Smithers—a man who's been with the party since before Leonard was in short trousers—of being too conservative in his approach. Called him an 'obstacle to progress,' if I remember correctly."

Mrs Liddell winced. "It was a heated moment, Mr. Graves. Debates can get passionate."

"Passionate is one thing, Mrs Liddell. But accusing a respected party member of holding us back? That's another matter entirely."

Dora's mind was racing. This was exactly the sort of information they needed. "Oh my," she said, affecting a scandalised tone. "That must have caused quite a stir."

Mrs Liddell nodded sadly. "It did lead to some... tension within the party. But Leonard was young and idealistic. He wanted to push for change, to make a real difference."

"And step on a few toes in the process," Mr. Graves added.

Inga, sensing Dora's interest, pressed further. "This John Smithers, how did he react to being challenged so publicly?"

Mrs Liddell hesitated. "John is a gentleman. He didn't make a scene, if that's what you're asking. But I won't deny he was hurt by the accusation."

"Hurt?" Mr. Graves scoffed. "The man was livid. I overheard him telling Leonard that he'd regret his words."

Dora's eyes widened. "That sounds rather ominous."

Mrs Liddell rushed to smooth things over. "I'm sure John didn't mean anything by it. It was said in the heat of the moment."

"Perhaps," Mr. Graves conceded. "But Leonard didn't exactly endear himself to the old guard after that. There were quite a few who felt he needed to be taken down a peg or two."

The implications hung heavy in the air. Dora and Inga exchanged a meaningful glance, both thinking the same thing: could Leonard's death be the result of a personal vendetta?

Mrs Liddell, noticing the sudden tension, tried to steer the conversation back to safer ground. "But let's not dwell on such unpleasantness. Leonard was friendly enough with the younger members. His enthusiasm was infectious."

"That it was," Mr. Graves agreed, surprising them all. "I may not have agreed with all his ideas, but the lad had spirit, I'll give him that."

Dora, seeing an opportunity to gather more information, asked, "Did Leonard have any close friends within the party? Anyone who might be particularly affected by his passing?"

Mrs Liddell thought for a moment. "He was still new to the group. His closest tie was with Miss Anita Thornberry."

Mr. Graves nodded. "Aye, that was another mark in his favour. It is hard to take down a man who has the support of both the leader of the House of Lords and is stepping out with the daughter of a major party donor."

The room fell silent for a moment, each person lost in their own thoughts. Dora and Inga knew they had stumbled upon a wealth of information, but it only seemed to complicate matters further. Who among these passionate party members might have had reason to want Leonard out of the picture?

Mrs Liddell, perhaps sensing the dark turn of their thoughts, clapped her hands together. "Well, I think that's quite enough gossip for one day. Shall we discuss how you ladies might help with our upcoming social events? It is short notice, but we have one in two days' time. Might you be free?"

Mrs Liddell launched into a description of the upcoming event. Dora and Inga pretended to pay close attention, though their minds whirled with the new information they had uncovered. It was clear that Leonard Thompson had been a controversial figure within the party, and his death had left behind a tangled web of potential motives and suspects.

As they left the Labour Party headquarters an hour later, Dora and Inga knew they had their work cut out for them. The case of Leonard Thompson's death was far from solved, and it seemed that every new piece of information only deepened the mystery. On the positive side, they had a new lead for Rex and Clark to explore, and an invitation to the party's next event.

Chapter 12
A Cad's Tale

It only took Rex and Harris a few minutes' worth of conversation with Clark to uncover that lack of interest was not the reason behind their friend's reticence with regard to Prudence. Though Clark carefully chose his words, his expression softened when he spoke about how lovely she had looked the night before. He got the far off look in his eyes that for Rex and Harris was a dead giveaway.

But getting Clark to admit that out loud took far longer. In the drawing room of Clark's townhouse, Rex motioned for Harris to take the seat opposite Clark. Harris put his years of police questioning to work, approaching the topic from multiple angles until he extracted a full confession.

"You kissed her?" Rex blurted, unable to stop himself.

Clark hid his face in his hands. "I know. I am an absolute cad. You don't need to say it."

Calling Clark a cad was the furthest thing from Rex's mind. He rushed to reassure the man. "That was surprise in my voice, not disgust. If you kissed her, and from what you said, it seems she returned the favour, why haven't you invited her out for a night on the town?"

"How can I when I am the very part of society she despises? If I take her to one of my haunts, I'll only confirm her worst suspicions. If I pick a place more appropriate to her tastes, she'll accuse me of pandering. No, Rex, I know you mean well, but it is not meant to be. Especially not now when the proof of my failures lies all around us. I would prefer to live with the hope of someday rather than get the no now."

Harris interrupted. "This someday? What has to happen to make it possible for you and Prudence to explore your interest in one another?"

Clark shrugged with a despondent look on his face. "Everything? Maybe in a few years' time, when I have proven myself worthy of everyone's trust, and am no longer at risk of making mistakes like I've done now. Prudence deserves a man who does everything right."

Rex and Harris exchanged glances as Clark ran his fingers through his hair. Rex had to intervene and fast.

"Balderdash!"

Clark lifted his gaze. "Eh?"

"If women required men to be perfect before bestowing their favour, the history of mankind would have ended with Adam. Look at the pair of us. Is Harris perfect? You know I am equally incapable of doing everything right. Yet here we are, married men, the both of us."

Harris added, "Perfection is boring, Clark. My Inga and his Dora are in their element when there is something to fix. Sometimes I make mistakes just to give Inga the feeling of having the upper hand."

"You do?" Rex was aghast.

"Aye, and it works like a charm, so I suggest you add that trick to your repertoire. Prudence kissed you back, Clark. She did not halt your approach and present you with a list of necessary conditions for winning her affection."

Some of the despondency faded from Clark's face to be replaced by a hint of hope. "You really think so? But surely she must hate me now. We have never spoken of it again, and so much time has gone past..."

"Yet, she offered to accompany you last night, and even allowed Dora to dress her," Rex pointed out. Clark tilted his head to the side and stared out the window. For his part, Rex was glad to see the man giving his words due consideration. After a lengthy pause, Rex added a final piece of advice. "Meet her halfway, my friend, and you might be surprised by what you find."

Clark, however, was not ready to fully embrace the idea of sharing his feelings with Prudence. "I will take your advice into consideration. First, though, we must find who is responsible for sending that poisoned letter. On that front, where are we?"

Rex shared Dora's and Inga's plans to visit the Labour Party office that morning. Soon after, Clark's butler came into the room bearing a message. He handed the folded paper to Clark and said the deliverer had declined to wait for a response.

Clark skimmed the brief note. "It is from Dora. She says we are to call on John Smithers, MP. He had a heated exchange with Leonard shortly before his death."

The name rang a faint bell, but Rex could not bring a face to mind. From the way Clark leapt to his feet to go, he wasn't having any trouble picturing the man. Of course, it was Clark's responsibility to keep track of the various members of Parliament, their affiliations, and areas of interest. Rex's task was to track those on foreign shores who might fall prey to the temptation to meddle in British politics.

Clark, however, had no plans to leave Rex behind. He urged the man to get moving and called for the butler to get their coats and hats. Harris offered to play the role of chauffeur, and they were off.

Clark gave the name of the Red Lion on Parliament Street as their destination. It was a favourite among London's politicos, and given it was nearly lunch hour, it was a safe enough bet that they might find the man in question there.

The Red Lion had once been a favourite watering hole of Charles Dickens. The installation of a Division Bell, on top of its proximity to Westminster, explained its popularity with politicians on either side of the aisle. They could step out for a quick chat over a pint and make it back in time to vote should the Division Bell ring.

Clark located John Smithers at the far end of the pub's main bar, handing over a few coins to cover his pint of ale. Smithers was a stout, middle-aged man with a neatly trimmed moustache and receding hairline, dressed in a well-worn tweed suit. Despite his years in elected office, he still bore the ruddy complexion and calloused hands from his start as a working-class man.

Clark hailed to get the man's attention. "Smithers, just the man I hoped to see. If you haven't got lunch plans, can I buy you a meal in exchange for bending your ear?"

In Smithers's shoes, Rex would have turned tail and run in the opposite direction, but Clark's standing in the House of Lords ensured the man stayed put.

"I cannot imagine what topic requires my expertise, but I would be a fool to turn down a free meal. By all means, yes. I have already put my name down for a table."

A waiter guided the trio to a table for four in the corner of the room. There was enough ambient noise for Rex not to worry overmuch about anyone listening in. A quick perusal of the menu and an order for the pie of the day all around later, the men got down to business.

First, Clark explained away Rex's presence by saying he was considering dabbling in politics and had come along to see exactly what it was that the politicians did all day. Next, he segued onto the topic of Smithers's Private Member bill that had defied the odds to get Commons approval and was now working its way through the House of Lords.

Rex had no reason to pay close attention to the particulars, so instead, he watched the men themselves. Clark displayed an awareness of Parliament business that far exceeded Rex's expectations. Smithers shifted from a surprised eyebrow raise to nodding respectfully in between answering questions. Clark kept up his questions in between bites of the steak and ale pie. He did not turn the conversation toward the matter of the investigation until they each had a steaming bowl of apple crumble swimming in cream before them.

"Smithers," Clark said, "what is the party's sentiment about the attempt on McAlister's life?"

"We are all horrified, of course. I would be of half a mind to suspect the Tories if it weren't for two things."

Rex paused with his spoon halfway to his mouth, more interested in Smithers's next statement than his pudding.

Smithers leaned closer and lowered his voice. "The Tories are smart enough to recognise that killing McAlister would make a martyr of him, and that won't get them any closer to Downing Street. More importantly, I am of half a mind to believe the dead man bears responsibility."

Rex shook his head in shock. "The clerk poisoned himself?"

"Not directly. But since the day he showed up in McAlister's office, I knew something was off about him. I did some digging and uncovered that he'd expressed affinity with the communist ideals during his university days."

Clark scoffed, "Young men spout plenty of nonsense while at uni, it is practically a rite of passage. Once they bump up against the realities of being an adult with responsibilities, they change their tune."

Smithers did not agree. "The boy took me to task—me!—for being too conservative in my ideas. After that, you can wager your last pound that I paid him close attention. I bided my time until the chance to have a look through his papers came to pass. I found a piece of paper, half torn, but I recognised the address at the top as that of Ben Bradley's factory. Either Leonard was a spy for the reds or he abandoned their cause and they came after him. Either way, I say McAlister is safer with him gone."

Clark whistled. "I say, that is shocking all around. Did you tell anyone of your findings?"

"I didn't get the chance before the lad was found dead. It hardly matters now, does it?" Smithers glanced down at his watch and frowned. "I hate to eat and run, but I am due at a meeting in five minutes' time. Much obliged for the free meal and the discussion of my bill. I hope you will lend your support."

Clark promised to give it his full consideration and then bid the man farewell. After paying the tab, Clark and Rex decided to take full advantage of the sunshine and stretch their legs. They ambled down Parliament Street in the direction of Westminster but turned left toward the Thames rather than crossing to go inside. They stopped halfway across Westminster Bridge and turned around to gaze at the impressive facade of Parliament's halls and towers.

Rex leaned against the bridge's stone balustrade, his brow furrowed in thought. "Well, old chap, what do you make of all this?"

Clark sighed heavily and then lifted his hand to smooth his moustache. "I'm not sure what to think, Rex. On one hand, we have Walter Philipson, the only communist with a motive but no clear opportunity. Only someone closely involved in Parliament would know that the clerks open mail, and not the members themselves. But would an angry Labour member kill him in that manner? They would have been better off taking the proof to McAlister and demanding he fire Leonard."

"It's a right mess, isn't it?" Rex groaned. "We still don't understand the significance of the letter used to deliver the poison. Was it really a coded message from the communists? Was it a fake meant to cast aspersions on Leonard?"

"Far too many questions, still. We are chasing shadows," Clark grumbled grimly.

Rex hated to see his friend so downtrodden. He had to do something to give the man hope that all would come out right in the end. He straightened up, turning to face Clark. "Perhaps Dora and Inga should speak with Anita again? They can ask whether Leonard mentioned the dust-up with Smithers, or if Leonard mentioned making any other enemies."

Clark shook his head. "How would Dora and Inga explain their second visit? The rest of the world believes McAlister was the target."

"Fair point," Rex conceded. "Then we speak with McAlister and Bradley again."

Clark's face darkened. "And admit we've made no progress? I'm not keen on that idea, Rex. I got them into this mess, and I've promised we will uncover the identity of the killer. If we go back empty-handed, we risk losing their trust and cooperation."

Rex could see the frustration etched on Clark's face. He placed a comforting hand on his friend's shoulder. "We'll figure this out, Clark. We always do."

Clark managed a weak smile. "I hope you're right. But for now, I think I need to sleep on it. Perhaps a fresh perspective in the morning will yield some new ideas." Clark hesitated, and then added, "Rex, about Lord Audley... I'd appreciate it if you didn't mention my lack of progress to him just yet. I know he's expecting results, but I'd rather not disappoint him until I've exhausted all options."

Rex studied his friend's face, noting the worry lines that had deepened over the course of their investigation. "Of course, Clark. But remember, we're in this together. You don't shoulder all the burden yourself."

Clark gave a grateful smile, but it didn't reach his eyes. Leonard's death was casting a very long shadow, indeed.

Chapter 13
The Cat Burglar Pays a Call

C lark woke in the middle of the night, but this time it was not because of a cat. Instead, a cat burglar stared at him, unblinking, while lounging in Clark's favourite leather chair.

Clark rubbed his eyes to clear the sleep and then revised his assessment. Though dressed in all black and wearing the satisfied smirk of Steinlen's famed Chat Noir, the beam of moonlight sliding through a gap in the curtains revealed a certain strawberry blonde head and emerald green eyes.

"Is someone dead?" Clark gasped, his thoughts racing headlong toward the worst.

"Only your spirit, darling man, which is why I decided to pay you a late-night visit." Dora, for it was she, lifted a glass to her mouth and enjoyed a deep sip of the golden liquid. A hint wafted Clark's way, confirming his suspicion that she had discovered his secret stock of a single malt Scotch whiskey long out of production.

At least she seemed to savour it, for she swirled the contents and gave him an appreciative nod of approval.

Clark, meanwhile, thanked the heavens that he had on his

Oxford blue silk pyjamas and was not in his altogether. Which led to another thought....

"Does your husband know where you are?"

Dora rolled her eyes. "He is hardly my keeper. But yes, he is aware of my whereabouts. You have no reason to fear he will call you out for pistols at dawn."

"My recollections of history lessons leave much to be desired, but tales of duels were one of the few things I recall. If he called me out, the choice of weapon would be mine. And I would choose something much more civilised, such as a dance-off at the 43."

Clark's remark caused Dora to throw back her head in a deep laugh. My word, she was glorious. And also, not his type. He pulled his mind back to the present.

"To what do I owe the honour of your presence?" he asked, sitting up straighter and fluffing his pillows into a semblance of a back rest.

"I am here to tell you a few tales... tales we should have recounted when you joined our ranks, but which we glossed over because you were present for all of them. Get comfortable, old chap, but do not by any means consider these as bedtime stories."

"I promise I will stay awake, though in the future, you might consider visiting at a more normal hour. Actually, wait a moment." Clark pushed back his covers and rose from the bed with his water glass in hand. He decided to ignore the fact that he was in his pyjamas. Nonetheless, his face flamed pink when he passed in front of Dora on his way to get a drink for himself. When he was back in his bed, reclining comfortably with a watered Scotch in hand, he waved for her to start.

"This story begins during the Great War. As you know, a certain bright young man and an adventurous debutante uncovered the identity of a spy in our midst. What we forgot to

mention was that one Lord Clark Kenworthy provided a key
piece of information. In a pinch, Rex turned to you for help, and
without requesting any explanation, you used your prodigious
memory for people to point Rex in the right direction. Five years
later, you offered your help again, coming up with an ingenious
way for us to steal a certain guestbook without raising
eyebrows." On and on Dora went, telling Clark the full story of
their shared adventures over the last two years.

Clark listened intently, though he could not discern the
reason why telling this story was important enough for Dora to
venture out in the middle of the night. He said as much when
she paused to catch her breath.

"My point, Clark Kenworthy, is that you do not have
anything to prove. Not to me, not to Rex, not even to Lord
Audley. You are Audley's mentee not because of what you
might do in the future, but because of all you have done in the
past."

"But I didn't know I was doing any of that!" Clark groaned.

"You say that like it is a fault. I view it as your strength. Your
instincts are spot on, Clark. You might even be smarter than I
am, and I do not admit that lightly. Stop asking us for advice on
what to do next, and instead let your gut guide your moves. We
all already believe in you. We all trust you. It is time for you to
trust yourself."

"I do—"

"No, you do not." Dora's voice took on a hint of frost that
reminded Clark of Rex's grandmother when she was displeased.
"You are stuck because you are trying to think like Audley and
act like Rex. Just be yourself!"

Clark opened his mouth, but no words came out. He could
not rebut a truth that rang so clear in his own ears.

Dora tossed back the last of her drink and set her glass on
the dressing table. She gave him one last hard look before

95

sauntering over to the window and climbing out. Without any goodbye, she disappeared from sight.

Clark hurried over to the window, fearing he would find his friend's lifeless body lying two floors down. Instead, she was skimming down the ivy trellis, her leather gloves protecting her hands from the rough wood. She dropped the last few feet to the ground, gave him a final wave, and then slinked into the shadows. No matter how hard he stared, he could not follow her path.

Angel and devil all wrapped in one, she was. Though she had meant well, Clark's head was no clearer for her advice. He was far too tangled in what-ifs and might-haves to discern the right way forward. His gut churned and acid burned the back of his throat.

He climbed into bed, but sleep took a long time to return.

Dora's words still echoed in Clark's ears when he arrived at the Labour Party event. The original plan had been for Dora and Inga to attend, as they had already agreed with Ellen Liddell. Further consideration that morning had led Clark to the conclusion that the event warranted greater numbers. When else would they find so many Labour members together, with drinks in their hands and a willingness to converse? And so, Clark rang McAlister with a request to add his and Rex's names to the guest list. Harris came along as well, playing the role of Mr Keble.

Everyone was in place by the time Clark's driver dropped him outside a large hall near the Pimlico townhouse. A conscientious young man in a dark suit checked Clark's name against the list on his clipboard and then welcomed him inside.

Clark stepped into the bustling hall, the low hum of

conversation and the clink of glasses filling the air. The venue was awash with a diverse crowd. He paused just inside the entrance, his keen eyes surveying the scene before him. To his left, a cluster of MPs and Lords engaged in animated discussion, their voices carrying the weight of political discourse. To his right, a more youthful energy emanated from a group of clerks and secretaries, their laughter and chatter a stark contrast to the serious tones of their superiors.

As Clark's gaze swept the room, he caught sight of Dora and Inga stationed near a refreshment table, perfectly positioned to eavesdrop on the younger attendees. For a moment, he considered joining them, but he remembered his responsibilities. He was no longer a young man, but a titled lord and member of the house. His place was with the elders. With a slight adjustment of his bow tie, Clark made his way towards the gathering of officials.

As he approached, he spotted Rex engaged in what appeared to be an intense conversation with Lord McAlister and several other men he recognised from the House of Lords. Smoothing his expression into one of polite interest, Clark prepared to insert himself into their circle, his mind busy contemplating how he could direct their conversation.

All plans fell aside, however, when he spotted a woman standing in their midst. Clark stopped so abruptly that someone bumped into him from behind. He spun around to apologise and by the time he had extricated himself, he found Prudence covering her mouth with her hand to keep from laughing out loud.

Rex must have noticed Prudence's reaction, for he turned his head and beckoned for Clark to join him. "Lord Rivers, come join us."

Clark composed himself and approached the group, nodding politely to each member. "Good afternoon, gentlemen.

And to you, Miss Adams," he added, meeting Prudence's eyes briefly before turning his attention to the others.

Lord McAlister smiled warmly. "Ah, Rivers, glad you could make it. Allow me to introduce Mr. Albert Thornberry, one of our most steadfast supporters." He gestured to a distinguished-looking man with greying temples and a neatly trimmed beard.

Clark shook Thornberry's hand, his mind racing. Thornberry—surely this must be Anita's father. He had not thought to cross paths with the man, but he meant to make the most of the opportunity to find out what the man knew about his daughter's relationship with Leonard.

"Now then," McAlister continued, "we were just discussing the party's priorities for the current term. I was telling Lord Rex here how beneficial it would be to have both of you officially aligned with us."

Clark gave McAlister a dry look. "Beneficial for you, perhaps, but I find it far more useful to stay in neutral territory if for no other reason than it gives me the excuse to sup at all tables. I will leave Rex to make his own decisions."

"Lord Rex's time is already spoken for," Prudence said, surprising the men by chiming in. When they glanced at her with raised eyebrows, she explained, "With Miss Laurent. I doubt there is any political argument in the world that could win out over her charms."

"Hear, hear," Rex said, raising his glass. "And there isn't a man here who would question my choice, either."

Mr. Thornberry, who had been quiet until now, spoke up. "I would be blind to miss her appeal, but a week keeping up with her exploits would see me bed-bound. Do not take this the wrong way, my lords, but I am glad my daughter avoided the fast set."

"Daughter?" Clark played the fool.

"Anita," Thornberry said. He pointed toward the other side

of the room. He gave a woeful shake of his head and lowered his voice, "She is here today with a few friends, though it took some convincing to get her to join me. She had been stepping out with McAlister's clerk."

"The one who—" Prudence gasped. "Oh, that is awful. The poor girl. Which one is she? I will make sure to speak with her and encourage her to come back again."

Thornberry gestured towards a group of young women near the refreshment table. "Anita is the one in the blue dress, speaking with Mrs Liddell."

Thornberry could have as well described his daughter as the one with the forced smile on her face that came nowhere near her eyes. She laughed along with the others, but Clark caught her twisting her fingers together. A nervous reaction, or so Dora had taught him.

McAlister said a few words about Leonard. Clark dragged his attention back to those around him, wanting to take note of their expressions. Downcast eyes and frowns abounded. Clark could not help but wonder whether he might see something different if he were to ask the young men who served as Leonard's peers.

He excused himself with the intention of wandering over to find out, when an ear-piercing tone rang through the air.

"Fire!" someone shouted from the back. The mood in the room shifted from jovial to terror struck. People crashed against Clark in their hurry to get out of the building. Clark braced himself, unwilling to leave his friends behind. He had walked only a few steps away, yet they weren't catching up.

He stepped onto a chair and searched for Rex's blond head. To his shock, Rex was moving in the wrong direction, going deeper into the hall rather than out the door like everyone else. Already the space was beginning to empty out, with Mrs Liddell bringing up the rear. Clark ignored her entreaties to go, and instead leapt down and dashed after his friend.

He caught up as Rex and Prudence reached the hallway leading into the storage space and restrooms. "Where are you—"

"There's no smoke," Rex shouted with a glance over his shoulder. "Not even a hint of it in the air."

"False alarm," Prudence added, not that Clark needed the additional explanation.

He could barely hear her over the blaring alarm. It grew louder and louder until it hit a fever pitch. The metal bell was too high above their heads to reach, but the metal handle to enable it was at chest height. Shattered glass sparkled on the floor, but much less that Clark expected to see. With great care, Rex reached in and flipped the handle back into the off position.

"What's that?" Prudence asked, pointing at a dark shadow wedged behind one of the remaining shards.

Rex used a finger to pull the item free. It was a crumpled ball of paper that, once unfolded, proved to be a political flyer.

A communist flyer, to be exact.

Clark took it from Rex's hand, folded it in two, and tucked it into his coat pocket. Though the Labour event was effectively ruined, the day had turned brighter for their sleuthing team.

"Why are you smiling?" Prudence asked in a wary tone.

"Because everyone in attendance was on the guest list. If there is another communist sympathiser hiding in our midst, we'll find them."

Chapter 14
A False Alarm

Outside on the street, Ellen Liddell made a fair attempt at holding the social event together, but Dora could see it was a losing battle. With upwards of fifty guests, the people pouring into the street clogged both the pavement and the road. Car horns and angry shouts urged people to move out of the way. Mrs Liddell's calls for calm and patience hardly made a dint against the noise.

A large group of young people decamped to the pub three doors down, while the party elders decided which of their private clubs to visit. Dora stopped one particular man before he got too far—the volunteer checking names off the guest list at the entrance.

He was easy enough to spot as he had the clipboard tucked under his arm. Dora bade Inga and Harris to wait for her and she dashed after him. "Mr Nelson, the clipboard. Mrs Liddell asked me to retrieve it."

Mr Nelson passed it over willingly and dashed off to catch up with his friend. Dora pulled the paper free from the clip and handed it to Harris. "Tuck this into your pocket. If that was a false alarm, and it certainly appears that way, we'll want to determine who pulled it."

Indeed, when Rex, Clark, and Prudence finally exited the building, Prudence made a beeline for the pair. "We found something," she whispered.

"Something beyond the blaring siren?" Dora asked.

"Yes—a commie flyer left as a calling card. Do you know what has happened to the guest list?"

Harris patted the pocket of his jacket. "It is safely stored away. We'll help Mrs Liddell finish tidying and then meet the rest of you at home."

Two hours later, the whole group reconvened over a tray of sandwiches and steaming cups of tea. Harris pulled the list from his pocket and smoothed the lines free from the folded paper. "We have the list, but how will we know who is the odd man— or woman—out?"

Clark matched his motions, pulling a list of his own out. "McAlister was kind enough to escort me to the party office where he provided the list of local members. The list includes their date of joining, matriculating university or college, and current occupation. That should be enough to allow us to make a start at crossing names from the list, particularly if we exclude all the longer-term members."

By the time the sandwich plate was empty, they had three possible outliers and one definite oddity.

"Anita Thornberry is not a party member?" Prudence asked as she grabbed the party roster to check for herself.

Dora waved her off the task. "Don't be so surprised. My father is a leading Tory and I'm not on their list."

"You are on everyone's list, but for a very different reason. One would have to be a complete fool to equate you with Anita Thornberry," Prudence fired back.

Dora fluffed her curls, not in the least taken aback. "True, but my point still stands. Children do not always follow in their parents' footsteps. You said yourself that Mr Thornberry encouraged his daughter to come along. He might be running a recruitment campaign of his own."

"Anita?" Clark wrinkled his nose. "You think she pulled the fire alarm and tucked the brochure behind the glass? She lacks the strength to break the glass in the first place."

"Not if she uses her brain instead of her brawn." Dora rolled her eyes at him. "If she packed something heavy into her handbag and whacked it against the glass, it would do the job. The glass is, after all, designed to break."

Clark conceded the point and sat back in his chair, suitably chagrinned at his mistake. He did not stay in that position too long, however. "There is one other possibility. What if we're looking at the wrong generation?"

Harris leaned forward. "How do you mean?"

"What if our alarming culprit is Anita's father?"

"Mr Thornberry was standing next to me when the alarm went off," Rex pointed out. "He couldn't have pulled it unless he had a magic watch to stop time."

"Who needs a magic watch when they have a full wallet?" Clark countered. "He could have slipped someone a few quid to pull the alarm, explaining that it was for the good of the party. You have to admit it is possible."

"Especially if he was aware of Leonard's past." Prudence studied Clark, her mouth quirked up in appreciation. "It is a somewhat diabolical plan, but it is certainly possible. Now, what do we do with that? Will you tell McAlister?"

Clark shook his head. "I can hardly accuse his biggest donor of playing false, particularly as I have no proof. I have the same problem claiming Anita is to blame."

Dora tapped a finger on her lips as she raised and discarded ways forward. Prior to the event, they had no obvious suspects.

Now they had two, though neither fit the main crime particularly well. She still had trouble believing Anita had anything to do with Leonard's death. If she pulled the alarm, she was hardly going to admit it to anyone. They needed more information, and unfortunately for all of them, she could see only one way to get it.

"We are going to have to watch them. Both of them," she added. "If Anita is involved with the communists, she's bound to speak with them at some point. Maybe she'll even go to a meeting. For Mr Thornberry, we are looking for evidence that he is willing to use underhanded methods to achieve his goals."

Surveilling two people's activities around the clock was a gargantuan task. Organising the efforts took some time and discussion and ended up involving every member of Dora's unusual household. Once the schedule was in place, they changed into appropriate clothing and climbed into their automobiles.

Dora and Harris had first watch over Anita. Harris took the wheel of the Model T. Dora, dressed again in her black cat burglar outfit, slid in on the passenger side. She issued directions to Anita's townhouse. They found a parking space under the deep shadows of a branchy tree and turned the car off.

The pair fell into a comfortable silence. Though Dora detested spending hours stuck in one place with nothing to entertain herself, she was capable of completing the task. Harris had long experience at the work from his days in the police.

Dora glanced his way. "What did you do to keep yourself awake on long nights like this one? Back in the day, I mean."

"I was a detective living outside of London, with no prospect of change. Building sandcastles in the air cost nothing but time, and I had that aplenty. I used to dream up elaborate fantasies about travelling around the world." Harris chuckled.

"Then Inga walked into my life, and the next I knew, I was on a ship bound for the continent."

Dora recalled his enthusiasm that first trip, bringing a faint smile to her face. "And here I am conjugating verbs in multiple languages. Remind me to ask you for daydreaming tips in the future."

Harris tilted his head forward, his bald head catching the glow of a streetlight, and gazed at her with arched eyebrows. "Your whole existence is a daydream, Dora. Please, for the sake of the rest of us, stick with the verbs."

The night air was crisp, and a light fog had settled over the streets of Chelsea, lending an ethereal quality to the scene. Dora and Harris sat in silence in the Model T, their eyes trained on Anita Thornberry's boarding house. The elegant townhouse stood quiet and still, its large bay windows dark save for a faint glow from a first-floor room.

Hours passed without incident, the only sounds the occasional distant bark of a dog or the soft rumble of a passing automobile. Dora fought against the urge to fidget, her mind racing with possibilities. Was Anita even home? Had they perhaps missed her leaving earlier?

As the church bells in the distance chimed midnight, a figure emerged from the fog. A young man, his collar turned up against the chill, walked purposefully down the street. He paused in front of Anita's boarding house, glancing furtively around before reaching down to scoop up some pebbles.

Harris tensed beside her. "That's Walter Philipson," he whispered, his voice barely audible. "Leonard's former best friend."

Dora watched intently as Walter tossed the pebble against a first-floor window. No response. He tried twice more before stepping back into the shadows of a nearby tree.

For a moment, nothing happened. Then, ever so slightly, the

curtain twitched. Dora's spirits lifted. Someone was home, and they were expecting this nocturnal visitor. It had to be Anita.

Walter, apparently satisfied, turned and walked briskly past their car. Harris gave Dora a meaningful look before silently opening his door. He closed it with barely a click and set off after Walter, his footsteps muffled by the fog.

Dora's attention returned to the boarding house. Minutes ticked by, feeling like hours, until finally, the front door opened. A slender figure slipped out, pulling a dark coat tightly around her frame. Even in the dim light, Dora recognised the graceful movements of Anita Thornberry.

Waiting until Anita had a good head start, Dora exited the car and followed at a discreet distance. Her black attire blended seamlessly with the shadows, allowing her to move undetected through the foggy streets.

Anita led her on a winding path through Chelsea, finally entering a small park through wrought-iron gates barely visible through the misty veil of fog. Gnarled oak trees loomed like silent sentinels, their branches creating a canopy of darkness pierced only by the occasional glimmer of gaslight from distant streetlamps. The damp grass muffled Dora's footsteps as she crept closer to the secluded corner where Anita and Walter met, their hushed voices barely audible above the gentle rustle of leaves.

"...can't keep doing this, Walter," Anita's voice, tinged with frustration, reached Dora's ears. "It's too dangerous. Someone was spying on Leonard."

Walter's response was too low to make out, but his tone was insistent. The fog was both a blessing and a curse. It provided cover for Dora to lurk behind a shrub without fear of discovery. The damp air, however, also muffled their words. Dora inched closer, careful not to rustle any leaves or snap any twigs.

"...pulled the alarm!" Anita said, her voice rising slightly. "What if they—"

There was a long pause, filled only with the sound of distant traffic and the rustle of leaves in the light breeze. When Walter spoke again, his voice was softer, almost pleading.

"Anita, please. Think of Leonard."

Anita's reply was too soft for Dora to hear, but the tension in her posture spoke volumes. After a moment, she turned abruptly and started walking back towards her boarding house.

Walter called after her, "I need you, Anita. We don't have long."

Dora pressed herself low to the ground as Anita hurried past, her face a mask of conflicting emotions. Once Anita was out of sight, Dora looked back towards Walter, but he had disappeared into the fog.

Her mind whirling with this new information, Dora made her way back to the car. Harris was already there, waiting for her.

"Well?" he asked as she slid into the passenger seat.

Dora quickly recounted what she had overheard.

Harris's brow furrowed in concentration. "I did not want Anita to see me, so I chose a position farther away. I heard even less than you did."

Dora nodded, her eyes fixed on the now-quiet boarding house. She balled her hand into a fist. "Dammit, Harris. Tonight's exercise has moved us a step forward, but I can't tell in which direction. When did Anita meet Walter? Was it before or after Leonard's death? Have we been on the wrong track this whole time, assuming this was politics gone wrong? From what I heard, it is just as possible that Anita and Walter were carrying on behind Leonard's back. Maybe Walter killed Leonard so he could have Anita all to himself."

"No, that doesn't feel right to me," Harris said after a

moment of consideration. "You had a better look at their body language. Did anything about their stances suggest intimacy?"

Dora scrunched her brow as she revisited the memory. "No. They did not embrace or even stand that close. But that could just as well be because they are on the outs after Leonard's death. Guilt takes a toll."

"We'll need to keep a close eye on her," Harris said, starting the car. "I suggest we add watching Mr Philipson to our plan. He is more closely involved in this matter than we initially thought."

As they drove back to Dora's townhouse, the fog began to lift, revealing the first hints of dawn. But for Dora, the mystery surrounding Anita Thornberry and her connection to Leonard's death had only grown murkier.

Chapter 15
A Call to Arms

Rex drummed his fingers on the steering wheel, his eyes fixed on the entrance of the factory where Walter Philipson worked. The car smelled of smoke, a remnant from its previous owner. With all the undercover work required by this mystery, the team had invested in a second inexpensive car. Used, of course, so that it would not stand out in any way when parked along the kerb.

Rex wished he had selected a space closer to the corner, where they might have found a hint of a breeze to clear the air. But he dared not complain, they were lucky enough to have an unobstructed view of the comings and goings.

"How much longer do you think we'll have to wait, my lord?" Archie asked from the passenger seat, stifling a yawn.

"Patience, Archie," Rex replied, his voice low. "Walter's day shift should be ending soon. We can't afford to miss him. Here, refresh your memory of how he looks so you can help me keep an eye."

As if on cue, a stream of workers began to pour out of the factory gates. Rex straightened, his eyes scanning the crowd.

Archie studied the rough sketch of the young man and then

concentrated on the crowd leaving at the end of the shift. "That him?" he asked, pointing toward a lone man shuffling at a slow pace.

Rex spotted their target at nearly the same time. Walter paused just outside the gate, lighting a cigarette. As he did so, a young man approached him. Rex watched intently as Walter reached into his coat pocket and discreetly passed him a small slip of paper. The man quickly tucked it away and hurried off.

"Did you see that, Archie?" Rex whispered excitedly.

Archie nodded, his eyes wide. "Yes, my lord. Do you think it's information about a communist gathering?"

"It very well could be," Rex replied, his mind racing. "Look, he's doing it again!"

Indeed, over the next few minutes, they observed Walter passing similar slips of paper to two more individuals—a middle-aged man and a young woman.

Rex's heart raced with anticipation. This could be the break they needed in their investigation. "We need to get our hands on one of those slips," he declared.

Archie furrowed his brow. "But how, my lord? He's not likely to hand one over to a stranger, is he?"

Rex chuckled. "If that stranger looked like Dora, then maybe. But for the two of us, I don't suppose he would. Fortunately, you have a particular set of skills that might come in handy right about now."

Archie's face lit up and he rubbed his hands together. "You had only to ask, sir. Best we wait until he pushes off. I'll meander past Walter and bump into him as if by accident. His pocket will be a little lighter with him none the wiser. Quick and clean, just like the old days."

"Old days? You lifted my cufflinks from my shirt last week and I didn't even notice until you handed them back."

Archie coughed to cover his laugh. "You were too busy

staring at your wife to remember I was there. I could have taken the hat from your head and tie from your neck, too."

Rex flushed. "Well, there is nothing here to distract young Walter, so best you have a care. Look, he's on the move. That's your cue."

Rex watched as Archie made his way across the street, weaving through the dispersing crowd of workers. As he neared Walter, Rex held his breath, silently willing his footman to succeed.

The collision was perfectly executed. Archie stumbled into Walter, causing the latter to take a step back to steady himself.

"Oi mate, watch where you step," Archie snarled, his voice carrying clearly to where Rex sat.

Walter righted himself and prepared to launch into his own retort when he got a good look at the muscular, blond man staring him down. Though Archie had a heart of gold, he was bulky enough to cause strangers to steer clear. Walter huffed, but left it at that, clearly annoyed but not suspecting anything amiss. His task accomplished, Archie carried on, circling around a nearby building to avoid being seen as he made his way back to the car.

Rex's heart was pounding as Archie slipped back into the passenger seat. "Well?" he asked eagerly. "Did you get it?"

With a cheeky grin, Archie reached into his pocket and produced a small, folded slip of paper. "As requested, my lord," he said, handing it over to Rex.

The slip of paper had only two words on it and a time. "Coleman Ironworks, 10PM." Rex scanned his surroundings, checking for that name on the side of nearby buildings.

"No point in looking around, as that old place is nowhere near here. It's in Southwark, or it used to be. One of the few places in London that didn't welcome the end of the Great War.

An old mate of mine worked there until it went under three years back."

Rex cranked the car until the engine caught. At a break in the traffic, he pulled out and then took the first left that would put them on the road back to home. "If we're going to sneak into a communist meeting, we'll need a change of clothes at the least. Since Walter has seen my face, I should ask Harris and Dora for help with a proper disguise."

"You could send me and Basil," Archie pointed out, volunteering his twin brother.

"We'll bring Basil, as well, don't you worry. I want to cover as much of the space as possible. At events like this one, the words of the speaker and mumbling of the crowd are of equal importance."

* * *

Several hours and one clothing change later, Rex and the twin footmen arrived at the former home of Coleman Ironworks. Rusting iron gates stood ajar at the entrance, creaking ominously with the slightest breeze. For a moment, Rex worried they had the wrong address, but then he spotted a glint of polished metal. He drove through the gates, following the weed-choked drive until the glint of metal resolved into a line of a half-dozen cars.

Rex kept going, choosing to park his car in the deep shadows at the far end of the lot. He backed into the space, planning ahead lest they need to make a quick getaway. The old ironworks building sat directly in front of them.

The view did little to inspire enthusiasm. The exterior of the factory was marked by weathered red-brick walls, now stained with soot and grime from years of neglect. Tall windows, many of them shattered or boarded up, stretched along the walls.

Basil curled his lips in disgust. "Who would choose to meet here when there are plenty of pub meeting rooms available?"

"People who have to hide their every activity from the public," Rex answered. "And let that serve as a reminder of the stakes, gents. If for a moment, the people inside think we're there to cause trouble, they won't hesitate to stop us... however they see fit."

Archie and Basil bobbed their heads in unison. Then Archie said, "Don't take this the wrong way, my lord, but perhaps you should stick with one of us, rather than going off on your own. If you let any of your crisp vowels slip out, it will be a dead giveaway that you don't fit in. We can handle the majority of speaking."

Rex raised no argument. Despite his efforts, he lacked Dora's ability to mimic accents. "I'll keep any replies short and leave the rest to you. Now, let's get a move on. The meeting has already started."

A faint hint of light bleeding under a door marked the entrance. Archie went first, with Rex and Basil bringing up the rear, and they found themselves in a narrow hallway. A gruff voice called for them to halt. A tower of a man with muscles upon muscles stepped out of a doorway.

"Codeword?" he grunted.

Ice slid down Rex's back and pooled in his bowels. They had not discussed how to handle any challenges this early in the process.

Archie pulled the slip of paper he had stolen from Walter's pocket and offered it to the man. "I don't know no codeword, mate. A bloke from my shift gave this to me and told me to show up."

That was, apparently, the correct answer. The strong arm

waved them on, telling them to go through the door at the end of the corridor.

The indicated door led them to the old factory floor. A line of candles lit the way through the maze of rusted machinery, long-abandoned workstations, and piles of scrap metal. The air was thick with the scent of oil, dust, and decay. At first, all they heard was the faint scrabbling of rats, but as they walked deeper into the forgotten factory, moving feet and a man's voice drowned out the rodents.

The communist sympathisers stood in a circle in the centre of the cavernous room. Rex could hardly believe how many people were there. This was no intimate meeting, but a gathering of nigh on a hundred. The man speaking was none other than Walter Philipson.

Archie tapped Rex on the arm and motioned for him to follow him. They went left and Basil to the right, placing them on opposite sides of the circle. Rex kept his gaze low. With his flat cap pulled down on his forehead and a moustache pasted on his face, he doubted Walter would recognise him, but he did not want to take any chances. He didn't look up until he and Archie had worked their way into the crowd.

Walter Philipson stood atop a wooden crate, his voice ringing out with passionate intensity. "Comrades, we must not be swayed by the hollow promises of the politicians! They offer us crumbs from their table, thinking wage increases will placate us. But we know better, don't we?"

A murmur of agreement rippled through the crowd.

"We seek not just better wages, but a truly equal society!" Walter continued, his eyes blazing with fervour. "The wealthy elite will not relinquish their power willingly. They cling to their riches, their privilege, while we toil in the factories and mines. But I say to you, their time is coming to an end!"

Cheers erupted from the assembled workers. Rex felt a chill

run down his spine again, this time at the hint of violence running through the raw energy in the room.

Walter raised his hands, calling for silence. "We must stay true to our aims, comrades. The road ahead is long and fraught with danger, but we must not falter. The capitalists and their Labour lackeys in Parliament will fight us at every turn. They will try to divide us, to turn worker against worker. But we must stand united!"

He paused, his gaze sweeping across the crowd. "And if they refuse to yield... if they continue to exploit and oppress us... then we must be prepared to take up arms in defence of our rights and our future!"

The response was electric. Fists pumped in the air, voices raised in a cacophony of agreement and excitement. Rex glanced at Archie, seeing his own unease mirrored in the footman's eyes.

Walter stepped down from his makeshift podium, immediately surrounded by eager supporters. Rex watched as the man moved through the crowd, speaking intently with individuals and small groups.

Archie leaned closer to those around them, his voice low and casual. "So, what's the plan then? For what comes next?"

The response was immediate. Suspicious glances, bodies shifting away, conversations dying mid-sentence. Archie quickly backpedaled. "Just curious, is all. New to this, you know."

Rex touched Archie's arm, a silent signal. It was time to leave. They made their way to the edge of the crowd, Rex's eyes scanning for Basil. He spotted the footman already heading for the exit and fell in step behind him.

They didn't speak until they were back in the car, engines running and the old ironworks fading in the rearview mirror.

"Well," Rex said, breaking the tense silence. "I think it's safe to say we've underestimated Mr. Walter Philipson."

Archie nodded, his face grim. "He's no mere rabble-rouser, that's for certain. The way he had that crowd eating out of his hand..."

"It made my insides freeze," Basil added from the backseat. "All that talk of taking up arms. Do you think they're really planning something violent, my lord?"

Rex's hands tightened on the steering wheel. "I don't know, Basil. But I do know we can't afford to dismiss the possibility. Walter Philipson is clearly a force to be reckoned with."

"What's our next move, then?" Archie asked.

Rex took a deep breath, considering their options. "We need to report back to the others, share what we've learned. This changes things. If the communists are truly considering violence as a means to their ends, it becomes more likely that they killed Leonard."

The car fell silent once more, each man lost in his own thoughts. The bustling streets of London gradually replaced the industrial outskirts, but Rex found little comfort in the familiar sights. The passionate words of Walter Philipson echoed in his mind, a stark reminder of the volatile situation they faced.

As they neared Belgravia, Rex spoke again. "Whatever happens next, we must remember that not everyone at that meeting necessarily shares Philipson's more... extreme views. Many are simply desperate for change, for a better life."

"You're right, my lord," Archie agreed. "But that desperation makes them dangerous all the same."

Rex nodded grimly. "Indeed it does, Archie. Indeed it does."

Chapter 16
The Betrayal is Uncovered

I n Dora's Belgravia home, Clark slammed his fist onto the table, causing the breakfast dishes to rattle. "Damn Ben Bradley for lying to me."

Dora picked up Clark's hand and coaxed his fingers to uncurl. "Do not blame Bradley just yet. Rex saw no sign of him last night. He might be as in the dark about Walter Philipson's plans as the rest of us."

Clark refused to be placated. "He is the party leader, Dora. He cannot afford to remain blind to what happens under the party auspices. If he doesn't take a vocal stance against aggression, people will assume, perhaps rightly, that his silence is approval."

Dora wanted to argue, but Clark was right. She had heard her father wax on about party discipline enough as a child to understand how critical it was to retaining a leadership position. If Ben Bradley was unaware, he was a fool. If Bradley was in secret accord with Walter, all Clark's plans to forge an alliance between Labour and the Communists were for naught.

It was time for another hard conversation with Ben Bradley, one where they could not afford to start off on the wrong foot.

Diplomacy was an art in which both Dora and Clark were well-versed, though it seemed Clark needed a reminder.

"Did you use those books I gave you as something other than doorstops?" Dora asked.

Clark's brow wrinkled as he eyed her askance. "I must confess I've had little time for entertainment, and even less for reading. By the time I finish the Hansard, proceedings, and various committee reports, my vision is blurry."

"Sun Tzu's Art of War is not a bedtime fairy tale, Clark. If you had read it, you would have an idea of the best way to proceed."

Rex raised a hand. "Wait, I know this one. Last night, Walter Philipson all but called for war, proving he has not read Sun Tzu either. If he had, he would know that 'The supreme art of war is to subdue the enemy without fighting.'"

Clark rocked back into a stunned silence.

"Perhaps you should pull those books back out from wherever you stuffed them. For now, however, let's put our heads together on what to say to Ben Bradley. If we approach with heated words, we will only get his back up. We must have cool heads and icy determination if we intend to get to the truth of the communists' intentions."

Dora suggested they approach the discussion as though negotiating a treaty. The first step was to identify an appropriate neutral ground for the conversation. She called Cynthia, her housemaid, in for advice.

Cynthia, as the younger sister of the footmen Archie and Basil, had grown up in the rougher parts of town near Bradley's factory. After a moment of thought, she recommended the White Horse pub. "Old Mick Brambles is getting on in years, but he doesn't put up with any nonsense. His wife Sue makes the best meat pie in London, although don't tell Cook I said that else she'll get her knickers in a twist."

"I will make you a deal. If you will ring and make a booking for a private room for lunch, we'll bring back pies for everyone and tell Cook she can have the evening off. If she agrees with your assessment, I bet she'll find a way to finagle the finer points of the recipe from Mrs Brambles," Dora replied.

"Ohh, I hadn't thought of that, miss. After I make that call, I'll see to finding you something appropriate to wear and set it out on your bed." Cynthia bobbed a curtsey and left the dining room.

Clark groaned. "You are going to make me dress in something from the ready-to-wear collection, aren't you? Let us hope no one sees me. My reputation has suffered enough by becoming a bore. I can't abandon all my pretences."

Rex rolled his eyes at his friend's ridiculous predicament. "Harris can drop you at the door and collect you there afterwards. Surely you can make it the few feet across the pavement without running into someone you know. Especially in that part of town," Rex added.

Suitably chastised, Clark nudged the conversation onto safer ground. "Very well, we have a place and time. Now, to the discussion. Let me think for a moment."

Dora and Rex exchanged glances, each making sure the other had taken note of Clark's request. It wasn't so much that he wanted to think as it was that he chose to find the answer himself. A few days ago, he would have turned to the pair of them for guidance.

Clark was deep in thought, oblivious to the secret smiles exchanged by his breakfast companions. He stared off into the distance, looking past the Georgia O'Keeffe hanging over the sideboard and into the possible futures.

When he straightened up and blinked to clear his eyes, Dora steeled herself for his instructions.

"Audley is not here, but I can hear his advice ringing in my head. I recognise the risks of telling Bradley all that we have uncovered. If he is already wise to Philipson's plans, he is hardly going to admit it. In fact, knowing we are on their trail may cause them to take action to stop us."

Dora studied her friend. "But you still agree we must speak with him, correct?"

"Yes, and I believe we can gain the information we need right now by focussing the conversation on Leonard. Now that I think back on our conversation with him, he never said where exactly Leonard stood on the matter of the future of the Communist party. He picked Leonard for his thoughtful nature. But what does that mean, exactly? That is what we must clarify."

"Well then, give the man a ring or, better yet, send Archie over with a note inviting him to lunch. I'll get changed into something more appropriate to our destination. Harris and I will collect you on our way across town."

Two hours later, Clark slid into the rear seat next to Dora. He tugged at the collar of his plain white shirt, unaccustomed to the rougher fabric against his skin. He wore a tweed jacket that had seen better days, its elbows patched with leather squares. A flat cap completed his working-class disguise.

Dora, for her part, had transformed herself into the picture of a respectable working woman. Her usually vibrant curls were tucked neatly under a modest cloche hat. She wore a simple navy blue dress with a white collar, its hemline falling conservatively below her knees. A worn leather handbag hung from her arm, replacing her usual beaded clutch.

As Harris navigated the Model T through London's bustling streets, the scenery gradually changed. The grand townhouses and manicured gardens of Belgravia gave way to narrower streets lined with modest brick buildings. Shops advertising cheap goods and pawnbrokers became more frequent sights.

As they neared their destination, Clark leaned forward, his eyes scanning the street signs. "There it is," he said, pointing to a weathered pub sign swinging gently in the breeze. The White Horse stood on the corner, its whitewashed walls grimy with city soot but its windows gleaming with welcome.

"I'll do the talking," Dora insisted before they climbed out of the car. She slumped her shoulders and shuffled through the open door, aiming for the bar. Like the outside, the interior of the pub had signs of wear and tear, but there was little of the stench of spilled beer and day-old food. Someone cared for this place, and Dora was willing to bet it was the hulk of a man behind the bar.

"Sit anywhere," the man said in a cheerful voice that still had a hint of his Irish origins.

Dora quirked her mouth to the side and pretended to screw up her courage to speak. She approached the bar, and in a hesitant voice that sounded remarkably like Cynthia, she said, "I rang earlier about the private room. Booking is under the name Clark."

Old Mick, for it must have been him, narrowed his gaze and scowled at Dora. "A private room, for you and that man with you? My wife won't put up with any nonsense, you hear."

Dora flushed to the roots of her hair. "Oh, it isn't for us. I mean, it is, but you see, my cousin, well really my da's cousin, is joining us. He's a popular gent. If we sit in the main room, I barely get a word in what with all the fellows stopping to speak to him."

Old Mick did not ease up his suspicion, despite her halting explanation. "Who's yer uncle then, lass?"

"Mr Bradley, from the factory across the way." Dora pointed vaguely over her shoulder. "He asked me to bring my fiancé to meet him."

Old Mick's face cleared at Bradley's name, just as Dora had

hoped. "Why didn't ya say so in the first place? Room's the second on the left off the back hallway. I'll send Bradley back when he gets here, and Mrs Brambles will follow behind to collect your orders."

They found the reserved room easily enough. The small space was dominated by a sturdy oak table, its surface marked by decades of use - rings from countless pint glasses, shallow scratches, and the occasional initial carved by a bored patron. Mismatched wooden chairs surrounded the table, their cushions flattened from years of use. Despite its modest appearance, the room exuded a sense of privacy and discretion - the perfect setting for a delicate conversation between unlikely allies.

Ben Bradley arrived a few minutes' later, failing at first to recognise the pair. Fortunately, Mrs Brambles followed on his heels to take their order. Dora kept up the show, telling her uncle how pleased she was to see him and making the introductions between him and Mr Clark. Without asking the others, she requested servings of the pie of the day for all three of them and tagged on a request to box a half-dozen or so more for her to take back home with her when she left. Mrs Brambles delighted in Dora's gushing compliments and promised to see to their orders herself.

When Dora, Clark, and Bradley were seated at the table, the latter commented on their unusual appearance. "You did not hide your identities last time we met. Why now? What have you learned?"

"We did not want to call more attention to our connection than necessary, thus the clothing and venue," Clark said. "Before I answer any more of your questions, I want to pose one of my own. Why did you choose Leonard to take on the role of McAlister's clerk? Did he share your aims?"

Despite what should have been an easy question, Bradley dropped his gaze to the table and fussed with his cutlery.

"Leonard was quiet, I told you. Willing to listen, and well-respected."

"Your reluctance to answer directly is an answer in itself, Bradley." Clark's sharp tone made even Dora flinch.

The communist leader jerked his head up and waved his hand. "No, no, it wasn't like that, though you won't like the truth much better. Leonard kept his own countenance. He sat on the side, watched everyone, clocked their every word and action. Before you take me to task, I will point out that me sending one of my lackeys would not have done us any good. I trusted Leonard to come to his own conclusions, and speak from his heart, rather than from what anyone else wanted to hear."

"Leonard isn't speaking to anyone now," Dora pointed out, causing the older man to splutter.

The arrival of Mrs Bramble bearing a tray of plates saved the conversation from deteriorating any further. The rich smell of buttery pastry mingled with spice and beef filled the air. Mrs Bramble set a plate before each of them and waited for them to taste it.

The meat pie was one of the old-fashioned kind, folded in half to make it easy to carry. Mushy peas and mash completed the meal. Dora cut into the pie, allowing dark gravy to swim out. She needed no urging to raise a forkful to her mouth. Though she had eaten in some of the world's best restaurants, she was in fast agreement with Cynthia's assessment of the food.

"Delicious," she said, bringing a beaming smile to Mrs Bramble's face. Clark and Bradley echoed their delight.

"Eat up then, and if you have any space left afterwards, I've got a sticky toffee pudding cooking in the oven."

Dora determined to eat every bite of her meal and a bowl of pudding, even if her stomach complained later.

After several minutes of eating, Bradley wiped his mouth and drank some ale. "Why are you asking me about Leonard's allegiance? Do you have some proof that he was planning to betray us?"

Clark set his fork down. "Nothing rock solid, or else I would have led with that. I won't say how or where, but we overheard a conversation between Leonard's gal Anita and Walter Philipson. It raised concerns."

"Anita and Walter?" Bradley shook his head. "Leonard kept those two far apart. In fact, he and Anita kept their relationship a secret from her parents until Leonard took on the Labour gig. That was the other part of why I selected him. He had extra incentive to make a connection with the Labour party work."

"Anita is not a communist?" Dora clarified.

"Not to my knowledge. She has never attended any of our events. I only knew of her existence because I happened to bump into the pair. Leonard introduced me and I recognised her surname right away."

Dora squared his answer against what she had overheard in the Chelsea Garden. She could only see two explanations. She laid them out for the communist leader and asked him which one was more likely correct.

"Anita and Walter went to a lot of trouble to keep their encounter a secret. Either Walter and Anita conspired to get rid of Leonard, or Leonard was part of their plans. Whatever those plans are... for we have no clues on that front. What does your gut tell you, Mr Bradley?"

Bradley pushed his plate away, the souring question ruining his appetite. "I hate to say it, but it is more likely Leonard was playing us for the fool. Walter and Leonard were thick as thieves before Leonard switched sides. His affection for Anita was not feigned." He balled his napkin up and set it on the table. "If you two will excuse me, I need to get back to the office. I will give this question more thought and let you know if I arrive at any different conclusion."

Chapter 17
Luncheon with Grandmama

Clark and Dora were barely out the door before the telephone rang. Rex was nearest, so he answered it himself. His grandmother's voice flowed over the line, tinny but clear.

"Rex, dear, I hope I am not catching you at a bad time. I had not heard from you about our weekly luncheon. If you are caught up in other matters and need to cancel, I will not be offended."

Rex had absolutely forgotten about all his obligations, but he was smarter than to admit that to his grandmother. That she would forgive him was certain. However, he and Dora relied on Lady Edith often enough to want to remain firmly on her good side.

"I was in the midst of putting on my coat when I heard the phone ring. I will be with you in half an hour." Rex wrapped up the call and hurried to turn his lie into a truth.

His grandmother was as regal as ever sitting in her Mayfair drawing room. Her silver hair, twisted into a tidy coiffure, was perfectly smooth, allowing the creamy lustre of the elegant pearl earrings in her ears to command attention. She still favoured the high neck and fitted waistlines of the previous decade, though she had allowed a hint of modernity to creep into the geometric pattern gracing the silk fabric of her day dress.

Rex took great comfort in the healthy pink of her cheeks. Lady Edith had been a source of comfort and advice for all his life, and he was in no rush to see that end. Perhaps that was why, in between courses, he chose to confide in her about his concerns.

"Don't misunderstand me, Grandmama, for I am as confident as any of Clark's personal and professional growth. However, given all that has occurred, I would be foolish not to investigate Ben Bradley more closely. The problem is, I cannot see how to do so without going to Audley." Rex paused to take a bite of his beef Wellington. "Audley would help, of course, but Clark might resent the intrusion."

Lady Edith sipped her glass of Bordeaux while she considered her grandson's predicament. "There is one other person in our circle who is bound to have reams of research into the communist leader."

Rex's brow creased but no amount of concentration produced a name.

"Your father-in-law," his grandmother supplied.

The fork fell from Rex's hand, landing with a sharp clink against the fine china. "The Duke? He is the last person I would tell of this."

"Pay closer attention to my words, Rex," his grandmother cautioned. "I said he would have information. I did not say we needed to approach him to get access to it. Think harder, my boy, and I am sure you will arrive at my point."

Not Dora. Not her brother, Benedict, another Tory leader. That left only...

"Lady Adaline," Rex blurted.

"Indeed. It just so happens she is due to visit me this afternoon. Given the seriousness of the situation, I am sure she will gather whatever you need, and her husband need be none the wiser." Lady Edith asked a footman to retrieve a pen and paper for her. She jotted off a quick note, added an address, and told him to wait for a reply.

Rex resisted the urge to give his grandmother a hug, as such things were not done at the dinner table. He did offer his hearty thanks and finished his meal with a much better appetite.

Lady Edith had not only requested information but had also moved forward her meeting time with Lady Adaline. The woman in question presented herself shortly after lunch ended, carrying an unusually large handbag. She was more petite in size than her daughter, but the mirth sparkling in her eyes hinted that the two shared a sense of adventure. After greeting Lady Edith and Rex, she settled onto a settee and opened her bag. Inside was a folder thick with papers.

"This was all I could locate in Stephen's study. He had them in a stack on his desk, so we dare not keep them away for long," Lady Adaline explained as she passed the folder to Rex.

Rex's grandmother suggested he excuse himself to the library, where he could peruse the contents without risk of interruption.

The Duke of Dorset's file had everything Rex could have hoped to find, from details on Bradley's financial state, to the health of his marriage, to his political history, both public and private. From an hour of reading emerged a picture of a man whom Rex could not help but admire.

Though Rex did not consider himself a communist—far from it, in fact—he was not immune to the suffering of the common man. No one who had spent time at the front lines should be, though Rex knew plenty of wealthy men who sought to put that time behind them. Ben Bradley understood the horrors of poverty from firsthand experience. He grew up living hand to mouth, one of eight children the family could not afford. The file detailed his career trajectory, beginning with doing odd jobs as a child, gaining fixed employment on the factory line, and working his way into a senior position.

Even his path to ownership of his current business was admirable. When the previous owner neared retirement age, Bradley had proposed to buy the factory, but he did not do so alone. Instead, he made every worker into a shareholder, giving them each a stake in the success or failure of the business. A workers' council made the decisions, with matters put to a vote. Though Ben Bradley was the face the business put forward to the external world, behind the scenes, the factory espoused the communist ideals of wealth-sharing and equal standing.

What interested Rex the most was a single page of notes in the duke's handwriting. Dora's father considered Bradley to be a radical of the first order, and a major threat to government stability, because of his success.

Rex's thoughts coalesced as he put the papers back into order and rose from his chair in the library. He understood why Clark had approached Ben Bradley with his plan to find a common ground with the Labour party. Any other communist would have likely shut the door in his face. Bradley was smart enough to see the value in listening.

But what of Leonard? Did his death help Bradley in ways yet to be seen? Or had someone outwitted the communists' ultimate success story? Rex could only hope Clark and Dora gained insight during their lunch.

* * *

Despite Rex's fervent hopes, his return home did not bring much clarity. Clark sat in Rex's drawing room, his jaw tight and cheeks pink with unspoken anger. The expression on Clark's face told Rex exactly how the conversation with Ben Bradley had gone. Dora showed no signs of being in a better mood. So caught up was she in her deep thoughts, she failed to even say hello to her husband.

"We had the right of it, I take it. Those closest to Leonard plotted his downfall?" Rex asked as he settled onto the seat beside his wife.

Dora blinked a few times as she drew her mind back to the present and then leaned over to buss her husband's cheek. "I wish that were the case, but I fear we have it wrong. Bradley discounted the idea within moments of us voicing it."

"But then why were they..." Rex's voice trailed off as his mind struggled to catch up. "Oh no. If they weren't against him, does Bradley believe they were working with him?"

"Yes, and that notion has left us all with a serious case of indigestion, despite the fine quality of our lunch," Clark replied, punctuating his statement with a pained groan. "Now I'm left to sit here on this settee while every theory I had curdles in my guts."

Rex had been in Clark's shoes often enough to remember that sick feeling. The only way through it was to keep moving, in both the literal and theoretical senses. He rose from his place on the sofa and used his foot to nudge Clark's old, scuffed loafers. "Come along, old chap."

Clark stopped rubbing his belly long enough to give Rex a questioning look. "Where are we going? And can I change into something of my own before we do?"

"Out and no. We are going to get some fresh air, and I would prefer no one recognised us." Rex began unbuttoning his waistcoat on his way out of the room. "Give me a few minutes to swap my trousers and coat for something similar to your own."

True to his words, a scant while later Rex hurried down the stairs to find Clark waiting at the front door.

"Why don't you want anyone to recognise us?"

"Because we are off for one of Grandmama's afternoon constitutionals, Clark. We are going to stretch our legs and our minds and see if we can't come up with a new way forward."

Clark shrugged his shoulders as if to say why not and fell into step at Rex's side. The men held their tongues for the first few minutes, giving the fresh air time to clear the cobwebs and haze from their minds. Rex took the lead, guiding them out of Belgravia and into Pimlico. He avoided the street where the Labour party office sat, not wanting to risk the chance of bumping into someone they knew.

When Rex was confident they were clear of any possible interruptions, he returned to the earlier conversation. "Did you tell Bradley about what Dora and Harris saw?"

"We did, though we did not reveal the how of it. Bradley flat out denied the possibility of Anita and Walter working against Leonard. If anything, he was as pained as the rest of us. For if he has the right of it, that would mean that Leonard was betraying Bradley. And McAlister."

"And you," Rex added. "You three are hardly newcomers to the political scene, nor to the possibilities of a double-cross. I find it difficult to believe that none of you would have caught on if Leonard was being less than honest in his dealings."

The clang and clatter of a passing lorry prevented Clark from responding right away. He held his tongue until they crossed the street and turned onto a quieter side road with less traffic.

"My initial reaction was to deny the possibility, but look at us, Rex. How many world leaders has Dora fooled with her French socialite routine?"

"That's different," Rex countered. "Women have almost

always been underestimated, a fact which Dora plays to her every advantage. My grandmother does the same."

"What about you? Or me, for that matter?" Clark shook his head. "People see what they want to see. Bradley, McAlister, and I all desperately want this to work. I never ever considered that Leonard might want the opposite."

Though Rex was loath to admit it, Clark's words rang true. The question now was where that left them.

The men walked on in silence, each lost in their thoughts. When their path took them past a small park, Rex elbowed Clark and motioned toward a lone wooden bench. Closer inspection showed the boards to be well-weathered, with rough surfaces hinting at years of use. This was a far cry from the manicured lawns of Grosvenor Square. There was no fountain in the middle where the neighbourhood children could find escape from the summer heat. The only flowers in bloom were wildflowers, their seeds sown by the winds rather than by hand.

Rex eyed the bench with some suspicion, torn between dusting it clean and the high chance of getting splinters as a result. He gave in to the weariness in his bones and sat down. Clark, ever wiser, fished a handkerchief from his pocket and used it to brush away what he could.

The men sat beside one another, feeling no need to fill the empty space with words. What was there to say now, when they were once again stalled in their aim of progress?

Rex raised a hand to his temple, both to massage away the tension and to urge his mind to figure out what to do next. It just made sense that the communists would be behind this. Why would anyone in the Labour party arrange a killing in their own leader's office?

Rex voiced the question aloud.

Clark froze in place and then slowly turned to meet Rex's gaze. "Egads, we have been fools, Rex. Absolute and utter fools."

Rex reared back. "Though there are plenty of examples of our youthful foolishness, I fail to see how bringing that up helps us now."

Clark shook his head in disbelief. "Because we are still fools. We have been so caught up in the who, we failed entirely to consider the 'where.'"

Chapter 18
Layers of Entanglements

Clark flagged a passing hackney, too eager to get to work on this new line of inquiry to waste time retracing their steps. "To Westminster," he ordered.

"Err, Clark..." Rex waved his hand, calling attention to their clothing.

"Scratch that. We'll need two stops, good sir." Clark rattled off Rex's address in Belgravia and then his own. The driver dodged in and out of traffic with the expertise acquired by long hours behind the wheel. When they arrived at Rex's house mere minutes later, Clark instructed Rex to meet him at the Lord's entrance in an hour.

"An hour? In this traffic?" Rex spluttered.

"You've got a head start on me, old chap. Are you up for this challenge or not?"

Rex scowled, which only made Clark laugh harder. He felt optimistic, for the first time in days. Optimistic because he was no longer wandering blindly in the dark.

That bright-eyed outlook hurried Clark through changing into more appropriate clothing. It spurred him to take the stairs down to the underground, skipping the mad chaos of clogged roads in the city centre. He whistled a jaunty tune while strutting around Parliament Square.

The guard manning the irons gates surrounding Westminster waved Clark past the lines of tourists and told him he had a visitor waiting ahead. Indeed, Rex stood by the specified entrance, deep in conversation with Benedict Cavendish, also known as Dora's stuffy older brother.

Clark was determined to go straight inside, where answers most surely must await. Benedict was having none of it. He stuck out his hand, practically obligating Clark to stop and shake it.

"Afternoon, Rivers. I am surprised to see the two of you here." Benedict glanced side to side, checking for eavesdroppers. "Anything I should know?"

Clark gave Benedict a good-natured clap on the back. "The cut of your trousers is six months out of date. Shall I ask my valet to recommend a good tailor?"

Benedict fell into a stunned silence, just as Clark had intended. His mouth opened, but no words came out.

"I'll have him give your valet a ring tonight, old chap. Ta!" Clark stepped wide, circling around a now stammering Benedict, trusting Rex to follow behind.

Rex did not catch up until they were through the door and halfway down the corridor toward Clark's office. "You are terrible. Incorrigible. There was nothing wrong with Benedict's suit."

"Other than being a boring, staid black, you mean," Clark countered. "I had to do something to distract him from further questioning. He is wise enough to our antics to realise the significance of your presence here. Another few minutes and he might have connected it with last week's incident. We cannot have that."

"Easy for you to say," Rex grumbled. "You aren't permanently tied to him."

"That is the price you pay for living with one of the world's most fascinating women. I, on the other hand, remain unentangled and am free to dodge conversations with whomever I like."

"Rivers?" a deep voice called out from up ahead.

Clark cursed himself for his previous statement. Lord Adams, Prudence's uncle, beckoned for him to stop. If Clark wanted to tangle with Prudence in the future, he could not afford to alienate her uncle. Even if Prudence was a grown woman capable of making her own decisions about whom to step out with, Lord Adams was the man who had stepped in to raise her after her parents' death. Though he was an uncle, Clark thought it prudent to treat him like her father.

Clark slowed his steps and ignored Rex's faint chuckle. "Lord Adams, how can I help?"

"Nothing urgent, if you are in a rush. Prudence mentioned your interest in my bill. I thought we might get together to discuss it. Perhaps over lunch one day?"

Prudence? Prudence brought up his name, at home, in a positive context?

All thoughts of murder investigations evaporated. Clark moved his hand up to get his diary from his coat's inner pocket. Rex intervened before he got the button undone.

"I'm sure Clark would love to meet with you, Lord Adams, but we happen to be running behind. Might he have his assistant give your office a ring to find a mutually acceptable time?" Rex asked, his face the picture of innocence.

Lord Adams nodded his head in agreement and waved them on their way.

"What was it you were saying about being free?" Rex muttered when they were out of earshot.

Clark took no notice of the teasing tone of his friend's voice. "She spoke of me to her uncle. What do you think that means?"

"It means you need to stop dithering around and ask her yourself," Rex replied. "The sooner we resolve our quandary, the sooner you can give her a ring. Now, are we going to your office or to McAlister's?"

"McAlister's, assuming he is in." Clark led the way through the long, carpeted hallways and up the various staircases until they reached the door marked with the Labour leader's title. The handle turned smoothly. Clark tried not to think about the last time he had visited.

He need not have worried. The scene inside was so wildly different from his last late-night foray, it hardly seemed the same place.

The first thing he noticed was the noise. Typewriter keys clacked, voices murmured in low tones, chairs squeaked as their occupants shifted around. Then, there were the people. A line of MPs and clerks sat in the chairs along the wall, waiting their turn to speak with the great man. McAlister's own clerks kept in a constant motion—filing papers, answering the telephone, and hurrying about on their errands.

"Can I help you?" a woman asked.

Clark shook his head to clear his thoughts and found Mrs Liddell sitting behind the desk. She arched an eyebrow, her gaze darting toward his hand that remained on the door handle. Rex was still standing behind him.

"Yes. I need to speak with his lordship."

Mrs Liddell's mouth softened. "There is a long line ahead of you, I am afraid. Would you care to leave your name and where I can send a clerk to fetch you when he is free?"

Clark was saved from replying by the appearance of an unexpected guest. The door to Lord McAlister's inner sanctum swung open. Lord Audley stood framed in the door, the office lighting casting shadows beneath his eyes. Though there was no way he could have foreseen Clark and Rex's presence, he showed no sign of being caught off guard.

"Excellent, Rivers and Lord Reginald, you are right on time. I was coming to fetch you." Lord Audley stepped back, making space for Clark and Rex to join him and McAlister in the latter's private sanctum.

They might have got away with it if it weren't for Mrs Liddell. She rose from her chair behind her desk and called into McAlister's office, "My lord, your next appointment is here."

Clark was close enough to see into the next room. McAlister glanced past Mrs Liddell, his gaze landing on Clark. Clark widened his eyes and bobbed his head in reply to the man's silent question. *Yes, this was urgent.*

"Something has come up, Mrs Liddell. Please rearrange my appointments for later in the week." McAlister glanced at his watch and then added, "After that, I say we call an end to the day. I do not want the clerks working after hours. I trust you can see they all depart on time."

"Of course, my lord." Mrs Liddell bowed her head and then turned to deal with the men seated against the wall. The firm set of her mouth quelled any thoughts of complaint.

Clark and Rex crossed the room as quickly as they might, with Clark in the lead and Rex left to close the door behind them. Clark sat in the nearest empty visitor chair, glancing between the two elder statesmen. McAlister had reclaimed his leather chair behind the desk, while Audley leaned against the bookshelf.

"Well, what have you learned?" Audley asked after Rex had also sat. "Given the late hour and lack of an appointment, I presume you are here on our shared matter of concern."

Clark had not thought to encounter his mentor, but Audley's presence was nonetheless welcome. In a steady voice, Clark gave a full update on their findings thus far. Or rather, their lack thereof. "After much contemplation, I have arrived at the conclusion that the truth of what happened to Leonard lies somewhere in this office."

"Here?" McAlister jerked back, the creak of his chair echoing his thunderstruck tone.

"It must," Clark insisted. "We know that the poison came from a letter Leonard received. How did the letter get in here? How did the sender make sure Leonard opened it?"

McAlister's stance shifted from shocked to pensive. He leaned forward, elbows on his desk, fingers steepled under his chin as he considered Clark's words. His furrowed brow and narrowed eyes indicated he was now fully engaged in puzzling out this new line of inquiry.

Rex directed the conversation. "How are duties assigned among your staff?"

"There is a hierarchy, starting with my senior aide down to the junior clerk. Leonard, as the newest and youngest, had the role of the junior clerk. Most of his duties were administrative—typing letters, taking dictation, running messages, and such."

"But I saw him in meetings," Clark pointed out.

"Aye, a few, and that was unusual. For reasons you well know, I brought him along to discussions I thought most relevant."

"Like the meeting we had on the day Leonard died." Clark cast his mind back. Leonard's sphinx-like expression had given no hint to his opinions on the topic. Was that because he was busy plotting activities of his own?

"Who took over Leonard's duties when he was out?" Rex asked.

"One of the other clerks, usually. If it is a particularly

busy day, Mrs Liddell sometimes comes in to lend a hand. She has a firm hold on the party's fundraising and social schedule, so my guests don't dare get on her bad side." McAlister gave a weary shake of his head. "I prefer to keep her in the party office, where I am less likely to accidentally step on her toes, but needs must. Like today—you saw how it is out there."

Clark fitted this new information into the picture evolving in his mind. Mrs Liddell had plenty of opportunities to observe Leonard. Did she notice what the rest of them had missed? Try as he might, he could not picture her as a killer. That did not, however, equate to innocence. Plenty of times, Clark and his friend had made that mistake, nearly letting a killer go free.

But he was getting ahead of himself.

Audley must have felt the same, for he asked McAlister, "Who filled in for Leonard on his last day?"

"I have no idea," McAlister answered. "The days, they run together. Should I ask her?"

Clark's sympathies went out to the man. The circumstances were bad enough when they thought the threat external. Learning he might have a murderer in his inner circle would leave a mark on his psyche.

Clark spoke softly, but firmly. "Do you have any messages saved from that day? We could compare the handwriting with others to figure out who covered the desk."

McAlister breathed a sigh of relief. "Yes, I am sure I must." He opened his desk drawer and scavenged through a large pile of yellow slips. He handed over all the ones from the date in question, along with some from today. "You check. I cannot..."

Clark took the proffered papers. The notes were short, nothing more than a few words to say who had called and what they needed. However, it was enough for Clark to notice the similarities. He passed them to Rex, who nodded his agreement.

McAlister's shoulders dropped. His expression fell, ageing him in a split second. "I will call her in—"

"No," Clark said, holding up a hand. "This tells us who might have put the poison in the letter, but not what happened to the envelope. If indeed Mrs Liddell is involved, she had an accomplice."

Chapter 19
Mrs Lawrence at Westminster

Dora was ensconced in her private study when a rap on the door drew her attention away from her book. The hidden door swung open with nary a squeak and Inga came inside.

"You had a telephone call. Mrs Lawrence is needed at Westminster."

"Really?" Dora's heart picked up pace. The men had learned something... if Mrs Lawrence was needed, that meant either Anita Thornberry or Mrs Liddell was involved. Dora put her money on the latter. "Are you to come along with me?"

"No, and Rex is on his way back. My guess is that Clark does not want to reveal the identities of all of us."

Dora understood that logic, but not why she had made the cut over the others. Fortunately, Rex arrived just as Mrs Lawrence was preparing to leave. He pulled a face at her choice of dress, but then kissed her hello on the cheek.

"Clark gave your name to the guards at the entrance, so they will be expecting you."

Dora gently caressed her husband's cheek. "That's lovely,

darling, but why am I going? Why not you? I am quick on my feet, but a little insight would not be remiss."

"You, my dear, are our body language expert. Clark is waiting for you to arrive so he can question Mrs Liddell... and John Smithers. That is all I will reveal now. I wouldn't want you to grow bored listening to their explanations of how and why poison ended up in Leonard's letter."

Dora did not stamp her foot, but it was a near thing. "You solved the mystery without me?"

Rex backed up a step. "Not all of it. It happened rather quickly, you see. Knowing how much you hate to be left out of the big reveals, I suggested you take my place at Clark's side."

"I do love the spotlight, but that isn't why I am frustrated. I am supposed to be the devious, clever one of the bunch, and yet I had it all wrong. I was certain the communists were somehow involved. But if Ellen Liddell and John Smithers did the dirty work, then the poisoned letter must have been a fake." Dora slid her coat over her shoulders and slipped past her husband. "I had best be on my way."

"We'll hold dinner for you," Rex called as she headed to the Model T. "Once Clark lays out the evidence, it should not take you long to extract a confession."

Archie was behind the wheel, waiting to make another round trip to Westminster. Dora told him there was no need to drive recklessly and added that she could switch to the Underground if the traffic was too bad. He assured her he would find a way around any snarls and then left her to her thoughts.

While Clark and Rex had been out for their walk, she remained home to contemplate next steps on her own. Her instincts insisted that Walter, Anita, and Leonard must have been up to something. But what?

Walter Philipson was a known instigator. She had no

trouble believing him capable of concocting a plan to damage the Labour party and the government in general. If Leonard was involved, what impact would his death have on Walter? In Walter's shoes, she would want retribution.

And that brought Dora back to the poisoned letter.

She had found the letter, still in the plain envelope Clark used to remove it from Westminster, lying forgotten on her desk. Taking great care to use gloves and cover her mouth, she had pulled it free and copied the content onto a clean page. Then, she had stared at it for an hour.

As Clark had said, the contents read like a page from a tale of intrigue and spies. Instead of dates, times, and places, the author had used various codewords. Something about it bothered her. The longer she stared at the page, the more that bother turned into an itch she could not scratch. There was a vague familiarity, but as to what, she could not say.

That was why she had turned to her bookshelf. She had been skimming through her library shelves, hoping something would fill in the gaps in her understanding. The telephone call asking her to come to Westminster came before any answers. Perhaps she should have told Rex to pick up where she had left off. She still could, she reminded herself. When the Gothic twin towers of Westminster Abbey's ornate stone facade came into view, Dora leaned forward and asked Archie to convey a message to Rex and Inga.

Her worries had not exactly lessened as she exited the car, yet they somehow felt more manageable. Was that not what Paul had advised the Galatians in his letters when he had encouraged them to share their problems with one another? The old minister at the family church had been right to insist Dora and her brothers learn this verse.

Now, she would turn her attention toward assisting Clark with his challenge.

The guard at the entrance offered to escort her to Lord McAlister's office. Dora knew the way, but Mrs Lawrence would not, so she readily accepted the offer. She played the wide-eyed, first-time-visitor to the hilt, giving an ooh or aah at all the right moments. Frankly, it was a nice change of pace from her normal routine of embodying a snooty French socialite who had already seen everything under the sun.

It was late enough in the day that few staff were around. Dora noticed a couple of familiar faces from the ruined Labour event, and gave a nod of recognition when they passed. She did not see her father or her brother, which she counted as a victory. It would be entertaining to see if they could recognise her in her current attire, wig, and make-up. She reminded herself she didn't have time for explanations if they saw through her disguise.

At the guard's knock, Clark opened the door to McAlister's office and stepped into the corridor. "Right on time, Mrs Lawrence. Please, come in. Jimmy, thank you for providing an escort to ensure she did not get lost," he added, before sending the guard back to his post.

Dora paused in the outer office. Faint voices came from the cracked door to the inner room, some lower in tone and another at a higher pitch. The conversation sounded congenial enough, at least from what little she could hear.

Clark approached, not stopping until he could practically whisper in her ear. "Mrs Liddell and MP Smithers are inside. We believe they conspired to poison the letter and then remove the envelope after Leonard's death. McAlister wants to know why, and nothing short of a full confession will satisfy him."

"Very well," Dora said. "I presume you will provide me with an introduction?"

"Indeed. I will take the lead. Your role is to speak up if you sense they are lying."

Dora inclined her head to show her understanding of her task. Clark's decision to include her now made sense. Ellen Liddell and John Smithers knew both McAlister and Clark too well to crumble at the first push for the truth. By bringing in a so-called expert, an outsider, they would be thrown off their guard. McAlister might not see through their lies, but would she?

Dora had spent years refining her knowledge of human nature. She had seen the best and the worst, observed consummate liars and those who swore to only speak the truth. Everyone had a tell, and few were better at spotting those than she was. Smithers and Mrs Liddell would find themselves out of their depths should they attempt to pull the wool over her eyes.

Clark rapped on the door to the office, causing all conversation inside to cease. The pair entered the room. Dora scanned the occupants' faces, taking their measure in a matter of seconds. McAlister was doing an excellent impression of a man in control, but his body hummed with tension that played out in the drumming of his fingers. Smithers took Clark's arrival with little fanfare. Mrs Liddell's expression went from confused to fearful to studiously placid at such a rapid pace that only Dora caught it.

"McAlister, this is Mrs Lawrence, my associate that I mentioned before. Mrs Lawrence, I believe you are acquainted with Mrs Liddell. The other man here is John Smithers, the member for Blackley and Middleton South."

Dora gave a brief nod of acknowledgement to each of them before moving over to stand near the corner. The position put her out of everyone's direct line of sight once they returned to conversation, while giving her an unimpeded view of their suspects.

"Shall I take notes," Mrs Liddell asked, pen poised over her notepad.

Lord McAlister sat up in his chair and forced his fingers to lie flat on the armrests. "Not yet, Mrs Liddell. Lord Rivers has been looking into a matter for me—a very personal matter. He is the one who called this meeting to order, so I will hand over to him."

Clark stood tall beside McAlister's desk, looking every inch the distinguished, titled man that he was. Proud, but not haughty, his stance was based on personal conviction rather than any sense that he was inherently better than the others. Ellen Liddell and John Smithers gave him their undivided attention.

"Last week, a man died in this very room, not by accident but by design. He was the target of the poisoned letter. Of this, I have no doubts. With the help of associates like Mrs Lawrence, I have sought the identity of Leonard's killers. Lord McAlister," he said, turning to the man, "the evidence will show that the two sitting before you are responsible."

Mrs Liddell's sharp cry weaved together with Smithers's spluttering, creating a cacophony of denials. All false, Dora noted with some satisfaction, taking in Ellen Liddell's wild gaze and the rising colour in Smithers's cheeks.

Clark was unmoved. "On the day in question, you offered Leonard a last-minute invite to join us for a committee meeting. Mrs Liddell stepped in to cover the desk. When the mail arrived, she sorted it, and in doing so, one caught her eye. She opened it and found a strangely worded missive. Rather than bringing it to your attention, she laced it with rat poison she found in the supply cupboard. Had that poison contained arsenic, Leonard might still be with us, but Mrs Liddell did not check, and therefore missed that it was cyanide based."

"Shame on you," John Smithers blurted. He leaned away from her as though her guilt was contagious. It was, but not in the way he meant.

"Shame on you, as well," Clark said, cutting in. "I came across the scene hours later, finding a dead man and a crumpled letter wedged beneath him. I did not find an envelope. Mrs Liddell was long gone home when Leonard died. So, I asked myself, who could have passed by to retrieve the envelope? An envelope that, I presume, had Ellen Liddell's fingerprints on it? I posed this question to the guards and they gave me one name. Yours, Mr Smithers. You were seen on this floor well after hours. You came in, made the gruesome discovery, and then made off with the envelope."

"Is this true?" McAlister asked. When neither of the accused replied, he turned to Dora.

"Yes," she answered. "Ask them why."

McAlister waved his hand in a silent request. Smithers had his jaw closed so tight that Dora feared his teeth would break. His time at war, and later in Parliament, had taught him the value of silence. Mrs Liddell, unaccustomed to the pressure of McAlister's fiery glare, crumpled.

"This was all Smithers's idea. Not mine. I wanted to bring this all to you."

"Bring what to me?" McAlister replied.

"As if you don't know, sir!" Smithers spat. "You hired a communist sympathiser and brought him into your inner circle. It took me one conversation to root out his true sentiments, and a week of tailing him to uncover his treacherous plans. I tried to warn you, to warn others, but you have had a deaf ear with regard to the communist threat. I instructed Mrs Liddell to keep a close eye, and to issue a warning if he stepped out of line."

"Death is a rather harsh warning, wouldn't you say?" Clark said.

Mrs Liddell burst into tears, and not the pretty kind that Dora employed to make men grow weak in the knee. The middle-aged woman's body heaved with sobs, tears running streaks down her rouged cheeks. "It was an accident, my lord! I thought he'd see the powder and throw the letter away. Or leave your employ. He was supposed to understand that carrying on with whatever he was doing meant suffering and death."

"There was one flaw in your plan," Clark said, with no sympathy. "Leonard saw not a threat, but a message from a trusted friend. He did not understand the significance of the powder, and thus left it to dig deeper into his skin. When he licked his thumb to help him better turn the page of a book, he sealed his own death warrant."

Mrs Liddell pulled a handkerchief from her sleeve and covered her face. Smithers, however, did not show a single sign of remorse.

"Despise me, if you will. Send me to the gallows, but do so at your own risk. The rest of the country will see me as a hero, for stopping a communist plot to bring down the government."

McAlister laid into a blistering retort at Smithers's bold statement. Dora's train of thought moved in a different direction. Had Leonard's death truly brought the threat to a close? Walter's flaming rhetoric and late-night meetings suggested that the risk of downfall had never been higher.

Chapter 20
To My Esteemed Colleague

Rex blinked to clear his vision, bringing the words written on the notepad back into view. After an hour of staring at them, he was no closer to making sense of Leonard's coded letter. He was working from the assumption that Walter had authored the letter. Knowing the identity of both the author and the recipient did little to help him understand the coded references. Dora had left scribble marks on the paper, circling some words, underlining others. As to why, he had yet to discover. All he had was the verbal message from Archie, to pick up where Dora had left off.

A flash of brown caught his attention. It was Inga, passing in front of the drawing room doorway. He called for her to join him. "I could use your help with figuring out the coded references in Leonard's letter. Do you mind if I read it out loud?"

Inga claimed the seat opposite him and motioned for him to continue. Rex cleared his throat.

"My Esteemed Colleague—

Our mutual acquaintance seeks counsel regarding the movements of our well-connected friend. He considers the following occasions but requires your insights to proceed:

- A visit to the door where Hyde once lingered, when the sparrows start their flutters.
- A quiet reflection at Tom-all-Alone's, as the pears begin to drop.
- A rendezvous near the inky river, when the knocker's last knock is heard.

Your prompt advisement on which rendezvous might best align with our friend's private affairs would be greatly appreciated.

In the shadows of discretion,
C."

He passed the paper over to Inga when he finished. "My best guess is that Walter and Leonard were collaborating on a plan to do something to McAlister—confront him, embarrass him, or maybe something worse. Walter wanted Leonard to check McAlister's diary. That matches with the scene Clark found. What I cannot determine is what dates, times, and locations the items referenced. Dora seemed to be making some kind of headway, but I cannot interpret her scribbles. Can you make any sense of them?"

Inga took the proffered page. After a moment of squinty-eyed concentration, she asked, "Was Dora working on this in the library?"

After Rex nodded in confirmation, Inga motioned for him to follow. They passed through the library to Dora's hidden office, where piles of books lay abandoned on the table. She sifted through them, glancing at the titles on the spines.

"I thought she might have been researching for whom Hyde Park is named, but all the books are works of fiction," Rex explained.

"Hyde Park's name is derived from the Saxon word hide, which was an area of land with sufficient resources to support a family. The area was listed in the Doomsday book as the Manor of Hyde, which you would know if you had suffered under the guidance of my governess, a woman so obsessed with the doings of Henry VIII that she should have been his ninth wife. He acquired the land from Westminster Abbey to turn it into a royal hunting ground."

"Keeping track of all Henry's wives was hard enough. So, if the letter is not referencing Hyde Park, what does the writer mean?"

Inga unearthed a book from the bottom of a stack and waved it in the air. "Perhaps a Mr Hyde, of the fictional sort. I don't suppose you were a fan of Robert Louis Stevenson?"

"I reread Treasure Island so many times that my father had the book rebound. He drew the line, however, at my attempts to dig for buried treasures in the estate gardens. But there is no Hyde in that tale."

Inga turned the book around so Rex could read the name on the cover.

"Of course! Dr Jekyll and Mr Hyde. I should have figured that one out myself." Rex took the book from Inga and flipped through it. "I'll skim through this to see if Stevenson names any specific locations, while you move on to the next item."

The pair worked in a comfortable silence, each focussing on their assigned tasks. When Prudence popped by to pay them a visit, Rex leapt at the chance to get more help. He told Harris to show her in and motioned for her to take the remaining chair in the hidden room. "Clark and Dora are at Westminster - confronting the poisoners, if you can believe it. Meanwhile, Inga and I are trying to make sense of this letter we found with Leonard."

"If you've identified the poisoners, why not ask them?" Prudence asked.

"The poisoners came from within the Labour Party. It seems they commandeered a letter from the Communist sympathisers and added the poison to it. We don't know whether Leonard's death is spanner enough to put paid to the communist plot. If it isn't, we must figure out what they intend —and put a stop to it." Inga pushed a copy of the letter towards her. "We've been working on the first two items on this list of places and times. Would you mind taking a look at the third one? Fresh eyes might spot something we've missed."

"Of course!" Prudence said, pushing up her sleeves. "I'd be delighted to pitch in."

She bent over the paper, her brow furrowed in concentration as she read the third item. A rendezvous near the inky river, when the knocker's last knock is heard. After a moment, her face brightened. "Oh, I know this one! The 'inky river' must be referring to Fleet Street."

Rex raised an eyebrow. "Fleet Street? How can you be so sure?"

Prudence flashed a cheeky smile. "Although novelists and bookshops are dotted around town, Fleet Street is home to journalists, editors, and printers. I should know, as I have visited the offices many times to meet with the editor of my gossip column. If there was ever an area where ink would run, it's there."

Inga nodded appreciatively. "Excellent deduction, Prudence. That makes perfect sense."

"And the time?" Rex prompted.

"'When the knocker's last knock is heard,'" Prudence mused. "That sounds like late evening to me. Perhaps 8 or 9 o'clock? That's when most of the newspaper offices would be winding down for the day."

Rex jotted down her observations. "Brilliant work, Prudence. Now we just need to figure out the other two locations and times. I'm working on the 'The door where Hyde once lingered' - Assuming the sender means Mr Hyde, my best guess is they mean how the story opens, with Hyde entering through a door in a seedy part of London. The location is meant to be around the corner from Dr Jekyll's home in a nicer part of town. I've worked up a list of bordering neighbourhoods in central London that might fit the bill."

Prudence tapped her chin thoughtfully. "That's excellent work, though we should consider that it might be a metaphor for a respectable place with a dark secret."

"I've pinned my hopes on it literally referring to a door in a less reputable area of the city," Rex confessed. "Either way, the time seems to be late afternoon. 'When the sparrows start their flutters' suggests around four or five o'clock, when birds become more active as the day cools down."

Inga nodded, making more notes. "Excellent work, both of you. Now, about the second item." They all turned their attention to the middle line, which Inga read from her paper. "A quiet reflection at Tom-all-Alone's, as the pears begin to drop. Tom-all-Alone's is from Bleak House by Charles Dickens. It was a slum located near the Inns of Court and Chancery Lane."

Rex nodded, impressed. "Any guesses on the time of day?"

"I figured that part out first. It was the location that took me longer. As the pears begin to drop is an old phrase referring to dusk falling. That must be early evening."

Prudence sat back, contemplating their progress. "So, we have three locations and times, but still no dates."

Rex cast his mind back to the night of Leonard's death. "Fortunately, we have a clue to guide us. Shortly before Leonard died from the poison, he went into McAlister's office and took out the man's diary. I suggest we do the same, and I know just how we can get our hands on it. Wait here."

Rex set his pen and pad aside and hurried out to the house telephone. He gave the operator the number for McAlister's office and then hung on the line, hoping someone would answer. To his good fortune, Dora's voice came over the line. "Lord McAlister's office. How may I help?"

"Mrs Lawrence, is that you?" Rex asked. When Dora confirmed, he continued, "Lord Rex here. I am so glad I caught you. I need to arrange a meeting with his lordship. Might you be able to assist?"

"I am certain I can facilitate such a thing. Did you want me to check now? I was just on my way out the door."

Rex couldn't help but give thanks for his fortuitous timing. "I don't want to hold you. It would be easier if we could look at his diary together."

Dora took the hint. "I will speak with Lord McAlister about your request. Leave it with me."

Dora rang off, leaving Rex certain she would bring the diary home with her. He returned to the hidden study to share the news. The trio spent the next half hour speculating on what the communists might be planning. Their theories ranged from a simple information gathering operation to a full-blown assassination attempt. Each possibility seemed more alarming than the last.

Finally, they heard the front door open and close, followed by hurried footsteps. Clark and Dora burst into the room, looking both excited and worried.

"Right," Clark said, brandishing McAlister's diary. "Let's see what we can find."

They moved into the larger space of the dining room and gathered around the large table, the diary open before them. Inga placed the decoded list of possible locations and times beside it.

Dora, her keen eyes scanning the pages, began to read out appointments. "Let's start with the afternoon time first, shall we? Here's something," she said, pointing to an entry. "Next Thursday, 4:30 PM, The Garrick Club."

Rex flipped open a map of London and checked the location against his list. "Leicester Square fits with 'the door where Hyde once lingered' seeing as it is a tightly packed square and very near the old slums of Soho."

They continued through the diary, finding two more entries that matched the coded locations and times.

"Again on this coming Thursday, at 6:45 PM - a cocktail reception at the Sir John Soane's Museum," Clark read out. "That could be our 'Tom-all-Alone's' - it's in Lincoln's Inn Fields."

"That makes this our last one," Prudence said, pointing at another entry, "Friday, 8:15 PM. I recognise that address. It is the Sunday Pictorial office on Fleet Street. That's definitely our 'inky river'."

The group fell silent, contemplating the implications.

"So," Inga said slowly, "the communists are planning something at one of these events. But which one?"

Clark mindlessly smoothed his moustache. "And more importantly, what are they planning? This is helpful, but it's not enough. But for the life of me, I cannot see an easy way to find out more about what Walter intends to do."

"Could you follow them around?" Prudence suggested hesitantly.

The others exchanged glances.

Clark sighed. "We can, and should, but we can't assume

that they will do something to reveal their plans. I hate resting all our hopes on luck."

Dora wagged a finger at Clark. "That might not be such a bad thing, especially if you ascribe to the philosophy of Seneca."

"The Roman?" Rex asked.

"Ancient Roman," Dora corrected. "Not someone we met on our last trip. He famously stated that luck is what happens when preparation meets opportunity. If we prepare properly and create the right opportunities, luck will surely come our way."

Rex, Prudence, and Inga were happy enough to go along with Dora's suggestion, but Clark remained unconvinced.

"Since we're on the subject of Ancient Rome, we would be wise to keep something else in mind. The goddess Fortuna brought both good luck and bad, with no guarantee of striking any kind of balance." Clark shifted his hand from his moustache up to tug on his hair in frustration. "We've got three possible events, each with their own set of challenges. We don't even know whether we are up against one person, two people— Walter and Anita—or a whole team of communist sympathisers."

Rex had to acknowledge the truth of Clark's words, but he wasn't ready to throw his hands in the air in defeat. "No matter how many we have to take on, I have faith in us," Rex said, scanning the faces of his friends around the table. "Walter, Anita, and Leonard may have put together a solid plan, but they did not account for one variable."

"What's that?" Clark asked.

"You. In any possible combination of Clark Kenworthy versus an opponent, I put my money on you, my friend. So, let us settle into our chairs and figure out how we're going to stop the communist rebels from bringing down the government."

Chapter 21
We're In This Together

Dora plucked an orange cat hair from the skirt of her grey dress and then dropped it onto the Aubusson carpet on the floor of Clark's drawing room. The man needed a cat. Or a dog. He needed someone to show him unconditional love and support, particularly during the moments when he felt nervous.

She supposed that this must be one such moment. Why else would he have asked her to stay by his side while he explained their very unorthodox plan to Lord Audley himself?

Not wanting to add to his anxiety, she tilted her head the bare minimum, pretended to glance at the grandfather clock standing across the room, and instead studied Clark's body language. She was, after all, the body language expert.

However, either her talents failed her, or Clark was not nervous at all. There was no sheen of sweat on his brow, shifting in his seat, or even a drumming of his fingers on the arm rest. He sat still, comfortably settled against the backrest of his favourite wingback. Yes, he was lost in thought, but not pained by whatever passed through his head. It was the cool confidence of his stance that prompted her to speak up.

"Are you sure you need me here?"

"Yes, absolutely." Clark met her gaze head on. "Sit tight and you will soon see why."

Lord Audley seemed to share Dora's question when he arrived a few minutes later. He lifted his hat, revealing his salt and pepper hair, and passed it to Clark's butler. He declined the offer of a drink and then took a seat.

It was nearing the dinner hour. Flames danced in the fireplace, just enough to ward off any hint of damp from the spring air. The drawing room decor was a strange mix of modern touches with more traditional furnishings. Clark had moved into the larger family home after inheriting the title but had yet to fully leave his own mark on the place. The dynamics were similar between Clark and Lord Audley. Dora's gaze shifted between the two men. One, the old guard who had unbent enough to allow her to join his cadre of spies. The other man represented the changing time, and perhaps a new way of doing things.

As for her, she was an island unto herself. That thought brought a hint of a smile to her face. She had long wanted to be viewed as an original. A better description would be a chameleon, for she changed the face the world viewed time and time again. A lucky few saw beneath that surface—and she valued them more than all the diamonds in the world.

But she was woolgathering in a moment when her focus was needed elsewhere. Clark was nearly done telling Lord Audley what they had learned. The test would come when he shared their plans for taking on the communist threat.

"Three possible events, you say?" Lord Audley asked after Clark finished. "The simplest solution is for McAlister to cancel them all, thereby rendering the threat null and void. But if that was your plan, you would not have Dora here with you. She has a habit of eschewing the safe course."

Dora could not deny that. Clark had no interest in arguing.

He steepled his fingers together, mimicking one of Lord Audley's favoured poses.

"I have thought long and hard about my decisions over these last few months. I still believe I was right to forge a connection between the Labour and Communist parties. My mistake was in keeping so much of our work a secret."

"Telling the world that McAlister and Bradley were on speaking terms would have been a gift only to their opposition. The Tories have been crying for the communists' heads on a platter," Audley argued.

"I made a mistake in keeping our plans to so few. It left a vacuum for others to fill. John Smithers and Ellen Liddell crafted a tale of a communist invasion and convinced themselves that they alone could neutralise the threat. Walter Philipson thinks Bradley a buffoon more interested in kowtowing to the Labour grandees than fighting for the rights of the working man. We can only guess at what he is planning. Even Leonard, the man at the centre of all of this, had limited knowledge of why he was acting as the bridge between the two sides."

"I cannot fault your logic thus far, but do not take that as agreement with whatever you have to say next," Audley cautioned.

That hesitancy had served Lord Audley well, all these years. He watched and waited, sending people like Dora and Rex out to dangle hooks in the water. If it took weeks, months, or even years for the fish to bite, did not matter. He would be there to reel them in and add them to his store.

Dora appreciated then Clark's dilemma. One ignored the methodical approach at their own peril. But the advent of technology allowed the world to move at a faster pace. Change happened faster, and perhaps even more violently. The Great War had seen allies turn into enemies. The negotiated peace had done little to cool the flames of injustice. Clark's nimble mind made him the perfect choice for juggling these challenges.

But only if Clark gave himself permission, first, and then demanded others like Lord Audley do the same.

"That brings me to why I asked Dora to join us. There are plenty of excellent reasons why we follow the rules. But Dora serves as a reminder that sometimes we have to bend them to suit our needs. The events in question will go ahead," Clark stated in a ringing tone. "We will not walk into them blind. We also will not go alone. I have asked you here to see if we can count on your support. Your vote of approval will go a long way towards convincing others to follow along with my plan."

Dora looked on as Clark walked Lord Audley through his strategy for the next few days. They would do the obvious things, such as setting a tail on Walter Philipson and monitoring Anita's calls. But other items veered into higher risk territory, including dangling McAlister as bait.

Lord Audley did not answer right away. Instead, his gaze shifted until he met Dora's. He looked deep into her eyes in a silent question. Did she agree with Clark's plan? Was she willing to bet her life on it? Rex's life on it?

Dora did not blink or shift. She held still as a sphinx. Lord Audley had to make this decision on his own.

The older man gave a dry cough to clear his throat and then replied to Clark's question. "Lord Rivers, though I am technically of higher rank, I do not consider myself to be your superior. I trust you to do what is right for England. You do not owe me any explanations or favours. I give my support freely. Now, tell me what I can do to help."

* * *

It was not Dora's imagination. Clark stood taller after his conversation with Lord Audley. He no longer suffered from the stooped shoulders in the immediate aftermath of Leonard's death. He had yet to fully regain his swagger, but she suspected that would come with time... and with vanquishing the remaining threat.

It took a full day to arrange for all the key players to have a private place to meet. Clark pulled a trick from his old scavenger hunt days, renting a private room in a pub where the owner could be counted upon to turn a blind eye. He sent notes around to the invited men, giving them arrival times that were ten minutes apart.

Dora came along to act as server. She wore a simple, knee-length black dress with a white apron tied at the waist. Both the dress and apron had been washed many times to lend credence to her role. Her red-blonde hair was neatly pinned up and covered with a small white cap. She'd used cosmetics to add shadows under her eyes and to hollow her cheeks. The tired fabric and exhausted appearance made her nearly unrecognisable.

She took up position at the far end of the bar, using a stained cloth to dry pint glasses. McAlister arrived first. He came straight over to her, as his invitation had instructed. She showed him to the private room in the back and returned to her post. Mr Thornberry was the next to show up, and Dora repeated her task.

The last to arrive was Ben Bradley. He stopped at the bar long enough to have a quick word with the owner. He handed something to the man, but Dora couldn't make out what it was. She added the dry glass to the growing stack and picked up another, feigning annoyance with the monotonous assignment. Bradley approached her, the only one of the men to take a good look at her. His eyes widened, and he opened his mouth, but he shut it again just as fast.

Dora motioned for him to follow her into the corridor. He waited until they were safely out of earshot of the main room before speaking.

"Ms Laur—?"

Dora held a finger to her lips and hushed him before he could complete the word. "What gave me away?"

"Your eyes. They sparkle brighter than any pub server I've ever seen. Are you here to help, err—"

"Rivers?" Dora replied using Clark's title. "Yes, not that he needs it. What did you say to the publican?"

"I put money behind the bar for someone who needs it in the future."

Dora estimation of Ben Bradley grew another notch, but now wasn't the time to show that. "Hurry inside. You are the last to arrive."

The private room featured an oak table, mismatched wooden chairs, and whitewashed walls decorated with cheap prints. Neither McAlister nor Thornberry seemed surprised by the identity of the remaining guest. Dora took orders for a round of drinks and hurried off to collect them. By the time she returned, the men sat around the table, with the Labour members on one side, and Clark and Ben Bradley on the other. Despite their seating choices, there was no animosity in the room.

Dora pulled the door shut behind her and then hurried out to the back alley. She and Clark had positioned a crate beneath a window. She climbed on top and then peered into the window he had cracked open for just that purpose.

"Men, we have a problem on our hands, one which impacts each of us personally. Bradley, a member of your party is plotting something. McAlister, you are the target. Thornberry, your daughter may be involved. We have two choices. We can fail separately or have some hope of success by working together." Clark stopped to catch his breath and then carried on. "Over the last twenty-four hours, I have used every connection, called in every favour, to figure out what the communist extremists are planning. I have found no evidence of any group effort. I've found no hint of anything at all. This is both positive and negative. We are likely not facing a riot, but we might be looking at an assassination attempt."

Thornberry scowled at Clark. "You think my Anita is involved in such a thing? All she likes is shopping and grabbing drinks with friends."

"Your Anita snuck out in the middle of the night to meet with a communist extremist. I cannot say for certain how she is involved, but they were not discussing their favourite department stores," Clark all but growled.

"So we ask her." Mr Thornberry crossed his arms.

McAlister stepped in. "She has no reason to be forthcoming with us. I do not want to see your daughter jailed. I don't even want to see the young extremist behind bars. He is passionate, if misguided. So please, listen to what Rivers has to say."

Thornberry unbent enough to take a gulp from his pint of ale.

Clark unbuttoned his jacket and took a piece of paper from his inner pocket. He put it in the centre of the table where all could see. "These are the dates, times, and events where we have the greatest risk. McAlister, I suggest you cancel whatever it is you have going on at the Garrick Club. Is that going to be a problem?"

"Not at all. What about the cocktail reception? It will raise eyebrows if I send my apologies so close to the event."

Clark glanced at Mr Thornberry. "I would like you to go with Lord McAlister, as his guest. I also suggest you two bring along the Met Commissioner. That will give us an excuse to have a greater police presence. If Anita doesn't hesitate to put her father at risk, hopefully the extra guards will discourage the extremists."

"That leaves the interview with the paper," McAlister said, studying the list. "Should I arrange for him to come to my office?"

"No, that meeting should go ahead as planned. In fact, we will make it abundantly clear that you are going into the building. We will arrange for the interview to take place in an easily accessible area and will leave the back door unlocked so our target will slip inside."

Ben Bradley raised a hand. "Hold up, Rivers. I thought you said you didn't want to see Walter go to jail."

"I don't. And that is where you come in. Listen up and I will explain."

The night air grew crisp, but Dora didn't dare move from her spot. She watched the three men's mannerisms, leaving Clark free to go over his plan and answer all their questions. By the time they prepared to make their departures, Dora was confident they would set aside their doubts and concerns and follow Clark's orders.

That was all Clark could ask, really. Leonard's untimely death was a terrible wrong. Sending McAlister to an early grave would not and could not make that right. But Dora hated that they had to pin all their hopes on their ability to make an outspoken, passionate rebel see reason on such an emotional matter.

Chapter 22
Ever the Hero

Clark had never enjoyed playing chess. He could not see the point of moving little carved pieces around a wooden board when there was so much more fun to be had in the real world.

Men like Lord Audley viewed his lack of mastery of the game as a flaw. Clark recognised the benefits. Instead of being locked in by rules about who could move where and which piece trumped the others, he saw life as a dance floor. A slide to the left, a swing of the hips, and a daring dip of the lady when you wanted to attract attention.

He applied those principles to the planning of their protection mission. Keeping McAlister safe was only part of it. He had promised Mr Thornberry that if Anita showed up, he would not let her ruin her life by getting caught up in the extremist plot. He had also assured Ben Bradley that if Walter behaved, no one would press charges.

Yet, Clark still needed Walter to make his move. If the man did, Clark didn't want to miss it. So he choreographed an intricate dance and assigned parts to everyone he knew.

Lord Audley pointed him toward a telephone operator who

could be trusted to monitor Anita's calls. Unfortunately, Walter never rang. That left the group with no choice but keep watch on the day.

Clark joined Archie and Basil for the first shift. Though McAlister cancelled his visit to the Garrick Club, Clark still wanted to keep a watch for Walter. He and the twins staked out the grounds, keeping a close eye on every approach. There was no sign of Walter.

Dora, Rex, and Lord Audley landed invites to the cocktail reception at the museum. They spun around the rooms of John Sloane's stately former home, pausing here and there to scan the faces of the crowd. Clark and the twins took up posts outside, keeping their distance lest they attract the attention of the police. Clark thought he caught a glimpse of someone fitting Walter's description, but he could not get close enough to be sure.

The team regrouped Thursday evening for a late dinner at Dora's Belgravia townhouse. The meal was served buffet-style so that everyone, footmen included, could gather around the table. They filled their plates with food and then took turns providing their reports.

"Anita accompanied her father," Dora said in between bites of roasted chicken. "He said she offered as soon as he mentioned his plan to attend. Neither of us knew what to make of it, though."

"Maybe she was there to protect her father," Archie hazarded a guess. "We've caught no sign of her meeting with the communists since that first night. Speaking of, Walter was also around tonight. I spotted him on the far side of the road, studying the place. He only stayed long enough to note the Met officers milling around outside before hurrying off in the other direction."

"So, it was him I saw." Clark pushed his last bite of roasted potato around his plate, mulling over the implications. He speared the potato, dripping with goose fat, and popped it into his mouth.

Walter's presence all but proved he had sent the coded letter to Leonard. Why else would he have turned up, or even known of the event? It was all going to come down to Friday night.

After dinner, Clark scribbled quick notes for McAlister and Bradley. He despatched them via Archie and Basil, giving strict instructions that the notes had to be delivered into the hands of the recipients and to no one else. They would proceed according to their agreed plan. McAlister's visit to the office of the Sunday Pictorial was to be an elaborate pantomime, with just enough distractions to hide what was really going on inside the building.

On his way home, Clark stopped at Prudence's flat. She had finally moved out of her uncle's home and into something more private.

Or so Clark had heard, for she had yet to invite him over. Even now, the doorman rang upstairs and then informed Clark that Miss Adams was coming down.

What would it take to gain her full trust? Would she always see him as the foolish boy he had been? Their chats were always too brief to give any hint of enlightenment.

She guided him to a low concrete bench tucked into a nook on the side of the building. An electric light high above kept them from being in the full darkness but did little otherwise to illuminate. They sat stiffly, facing forward, neither daring to so much as glance at one another.

"We proceed as planned," Clark said in a low tone. "You made the necessary arrangements on your side?"

"Of course." She stopped there, letting the rumble of passing cars fill the space. "Did you need anything else?"

No. *Yes.* Clark pressed his lips together to keep from blurting out that he wanted her friendship, respect—attention, anything but this cold awkwardness that lay between them.

"No. We have done all we can. I should let you get your rest." He rose from the bench and smoothed the wrinkles from his trousers.

Prudence's hand shot out. Her fingers grazed his arm. He jerked his head around, bringing their gazes clashing together.

"Clark... be careful, okay?" she whispered.

Clark searched her face for some hint of her emotions. The weak light left half her features hid in shadows. It didn't matter. He knew the curve of her cheek, her pert nose, the arched brow with which she judged and found him wanting. His mind's eye filled in the missing features, but there was one thing it could not reveal. Neither it nor he had any idea what lay in her heart.

He held still, rejoicing in the faint touch of her fingertips on his arm. The silence stretched to an uncomfortable length. What would happen if he leaned down and brushed his lips against hers?

He was too terrified to find out. He let his arm drop, pulling away from hers, and simply nodded his agreement. Then, he put one foot in front of the other, keeping his concentration on not looking back.

* * *

Friday dawned with a deep layer of fog obscuring the skyline. By noon, the fog had given way to a steady drizzle.

Clark woke and dressed as usual. He strolled into Westminster with a smile on his face that didn't quite reach his eyes. He made up for it with a garrulous attitude. He lunched in the Lords' dining room, then went for drinks at his club. At seven PM, when talk turned to dinner, he begged off.

Harris was waiting outside in the Model T. He flashed the lights twice before pulling out. Clark picked up his pace until he reached the edge of a narrow alley. Moments later, the Model T turned into it from the opposite end. Harris slowed to give Clark time to climb in.

They were both too focused to engage in idle chitchat. Harris navigated the busy streets, arriving at Ben Bradley's home at a quarter to eight. Bradley, with his hat pulled down low, joined them in the car. Off again, Harris drove them to a side entrance of the building the Sunday Pictorial called home. Clark and the Communist leader gave a staccato trio of knocks on the door to identify themselves.

Prudence let them in.

Clark did not dare allow his focus to shift as she guided them through empty corridors. She left them at the door marked FR Sanderson, Editor-in-Chief.

A gruff voice called for them to enter.

Inside, chaos reigned supreme. Papers scattered across every surface, ranging from handwritten notes to fresh off the printing press. Wooden legs suggested the presence of a table and a desk, but finding either under the mounds would be a Herculean task. Clark was so engrossed in making sense of the mess that he overlooked the man helming the paper.

To be fair, he was easy to miss. Between his pasty white skin and steel wool hair, he blended right in with the newsprint. It wasn't until he rose from his chair that Clark remembered why they were there.

"Lord Rivers, Mr Bradley, it is a pleasure to meet you," Mr Sanderson said. "Particularly you, Mr Bradley. You're notoriously reticent to speak with members of my profession."

Ben Bradley stuck out his hand for a handshake. "Do I sense a possible sympathiser to my cause?"

"You sense a man with pages to fill on a weekly basis. I'm a fan of communism, political strife, youthful antics of the Bright Young set, and anything else which causes readers to open their pocketbooks." The editor barked a laugh before sobering. "Which brings us to your rather unusual request. Miss Adams has dangled an exclusive interview with you and Lord McAlister. Together."

"At our request," Bradley explained. "We have let the Tories brand us with their slanderous lies for long enough. We are willing to grant your paper an exclusive, on two conditions."

"The first I understand and am delighted to offer. We will run the story this weekend. But the second makes little sense." The editor wiggled his eyebrows. "Care to explain it?"

"There is nothing to explain. If a man arrives asking for Lord McAlister, you are to show him to us and leave us to speak with him. In private," he added. "No one is to mention my presence."

When Bradley failed to elaborate, the editor abandoned his attempts to extract more information and showed them to a small meeting room. The room had a single round table and four chairs placed at even intervals around it. Framed versions of past front pages decorated the otherwise plain white walls.

When Clark and Ben Bradley were alone, Clark confessed, "I had hoped for something larger."

"This is better," the Communist leader said. "We have nothing to hide and nothing to fear."

Clark prayed the man was right.

The space shrank further when Lord McAlister joined them. He shook their hands and then hung his coat and hat on the back of his chair.

"Any sign of him?" Clark asked.

"There was a chap watching from a doorway across the street. It could have been him." McAlister settled into his chair with a groan. "One way or another, this ends tonight. If young

Walter doesn't make an appearance, we will use the paper to communicate with him."

Given the complexity of their plans, they had all agreed on a simple solution: a conversation, ideally face-to-face, to correct the misconceptions about what McAlister and Bradley intended.

As promised, the newspaper staff left the three entirely alone, not even an offer of a glass of water or cup of tea. They were to be undisturbed for half an hour, the only exception made if their visitor showed up.

Clark watched the minutes tick by on the old-fashioned pocket watch he had inherited from his father. He liked the idea that the old earl might be keeping an eye on him. He could use all the help he could get. If there was such a thing as a guardian angel, whoever had to watch over him had probably long since abandoned post after enduring years of Clark's wilder antics. Though he still keenly felt his father's loss, he took heart imaging the old man cheering him on from the beyond.

The knob turned at minute twenty-eight. Clark was certain his watch was off until a man in an ill-fitting suit entered the room. The suit had belonged to Leonard. Clark remembered him wearing it.

Clark, Bradley, and McAlister had chosen their seats well. The first man Walter saw was the leader of the House of Lords. His hand twitched towards his pocket.

"Sit down, Walter," Bradley said. "We've been expecting you."

Walter flinched at his mentor's voice but quickly regained control. "So you've come together. I should have expected it."

"We came because we read the letter you sent to Leonard. We could have acted sooner but we wanted to meet you on a neutral ground. Now, please, sit." Bradley used his foot to push out the remaining chair.

Walter was having none of it. He kicked out his leg to shove the chair back into place with such force that the other men jumped in their seats. He delighted in catching them off guard.

"I didn't come here to talk. That's all you lot do—yammer on about this and that. Meanwhile, men like me suffer." Walter's smile twisted into a glower. "Leonard told me all about your debates. Hours and hours of talk with nothing to show for it."

"I'm surprised to hear that Leonard characterised things that way," Bradley argued. "He was happy to venture into Westminster."

"Aye, he had stars in his eyes for a while, but I brought him back to Earth. Time dragged on, proving the truth in my words. Then you lot killed him. The bobbies pretend to look into the matter, but you put champagne in their hands and the search goes nowhere."

"That isn't true—" McAlister began.

"Shut up!" Walter growled, cutting McAlister off. He pulled a gun from his coat pocket and pointed it at them.

McAlister shrank lower, making himself as small a target as possible. Ben Bradley, however, was not ready to give up.

"We caught Leonard's killers," he said in a soft, calm voice. "You can still put the gun away and leave. Or, sit with us, and we will tell you how the murderers will be held to account. It isn't too late for you."

Walter cocked the gun. His hand did not waver.

For Clark, time slowed to a crawl. He could see all the possible outcomes. McAlister dead. Bradley dead.

Walter had hardly glanced his way. Clark was the nearest to him, yet Walter's main focus remained on the others.

Clark had made so many promises. Not one of them ended in another death. It mattered not who pulled the trigger or where the bullet stopped. Clark would forever hold himself responsible.

The responsibility that had weighed on his shoulders since the moment he found Leonard's lifeless body settled in. It sank beneath the surface of his skin, filling his muscles with strength, and hardening his bones against the icy fear sliding down his spine.

He moved.

He launched out of his chair, reaching for the gun. Walter lurched sideways, shock bleaching his florid face. Clark's fingers slid across the metal barrel. He pushed down with all his might. He heard the report of the gun blast before the burn on his hand could make itself known.

But that paled in comparison to the rush of agony that accompanied the scent of blood.

Chapter 23
Loose Ends Tied

Rex handed his coat and hat to Lord Audley's butler and then strode through the open study door. Lord Audley sat behind the ornately carved wooden monstrosity that served as his workspace. He finished the last few lines on the paper before him and did not raise his head until his pen rested beside it.

"Rivers?"

"Is going to be fine," Rex supplied while laying claim to a visitor's chair. "Though he won't be jiving on the floor of the 43 anytime soon. The shot fractured his tibia. The doctor says there is a good chance of a full recovery, or at worst, a slight limp."

"Heaven help us if he requires the use of a cane. He'll undoubtedly select something more frivolous than practical and delight in tripping up the young swains trying their hands with the secretaries at Parliament."

Rex chuckled at the image that statement brought to mind, but soon sobered. "He has earned the right to do that and more."

"Indeed." Lord Audley steepled his fingers together and

adopted his favourite stance. "Are you here to assuage your curiosity or his?"

"Both?" Rex shrugged his shoulders. "I rushed to the hospital as soon as Prudence called and have barely left Clark's bedside in the day since. We all want to know what happened to Walter, whether Anita was involved, and whether Mrs Liddell and Smithers will be punished."

Lord Audley dropped his stone facade at Rex's long string of questions and actually allowed a hint of a smile to crinkle his eyes. "I am surprised that your wife isn't here demanding answers, as well."

"One of us had to stay with Clark, sir. Left alone, he distracts every nurse and doctor with his endless tales of his youthful days. I stepped out for a quick bite and came back to find him organising a scavenger hunt on the surgical floor. For once, Dora and I are having to play the heavy and send people back to work."

At that, Lord Audley's shoulders shook with unvoiced laughter. He harrumphed and straightened the papers on his desk until he was back in control of himself. "Remind the good earl that he is a member of the House of Lords and a certain level of decorum is expected at all times."

Rex arched an eyebrow. As if such a threat would be enough to stifle Clark's renewed zest for life.

"Let's move on, shall we?" Lord Audley asked. "I will start with Walter Philipson. McAlister was initially keen to throw him into the tower, but Bradley made an excellent point. Walter is a hale, young lad in need of an audience. If we put him in prison, he will undoubtedly provoke an uprising within a month. Therefore, a more unusual solution was required."

Rex sat up straighter, his interest piqued. "Oh?"

"Lord McAlister has a large estate in the Scottish Highlands. He happened to be in need of a groom for his stables. Two of them, to be exact. Walter Philipson has agreed to a five-year term of work there in exchange for avoiding the risk of many more years in prison. At his young age, five years will pass in the blink of an eye."

"You said two grooms," Rex pointed out.

"I did. John Smithers will accompany him for the first year. The two will share a room in the house, take meals together, and work beside one another. They will be the only two Englishmen in a sea of Scots. Either they will find a way to see eye-to-eye on something, or they will have to learn Gaelic if they want to converse with anyone else."

"Oh, Clark will like this solution, indeed," Rex said. Clark's vision of bringing the Labour and Communist members together in discussion would happen one way or another. "I assume it is acceptable for me to share this with him."

"You may," Lord Audley said. He added, "But not within earshot of anyone else. We are working outside the normal course of justice and it does us no good to publicise it."

Rex gave a nod of understanding. "What of Anita and Mrs Liddell?"

"Anita has come out of this scrape having learned a valuable lesson. She did not know what Leonard and Walter had planned, though she was aware they were in communication. Walter approached her after Leonard's death to ask her help in checking McAlister's schedule. In the end, she found she could not bring herself to use her father's connection to facilitate something possibly illegal. She thought her silence would put an end to Walter's plans."

"Where there is a will, there is a way, at least where Walter is concerned. I do not envy Anita that lesson. It must be a bitter pill to swallow, especially since she lost Leonard as a result of his actions." Rex sighed heavily. "Poor girl. As for Mrs Liddell, I find I cannot summon the same level of sympathy."

"Nor can I," Audley agreed. "She, too, received a unique punishment. She will be volunteering at a small, private facility in Devon, one set aside for the care of men who suffered from gas poisoning during the Great War. Hopefully a few years spent seeing the damage poison can do to a body will prevent her from every taking such a foolish action again."

Rex had to give it to Lord Audley. Though only a little more than a day had passed since the incident at the newspaper office, the spymaster had taken all the loose ends and tied them into a neat bow. He had presented them to Rex like a wrapped present ready for delivery to their wounded hero.

This was one task Rex was more than happy to take on.

"Is there anything else you need from me?" Rex asked, preparing to leave.

"Yes. Can you find out how soon Rivers will be clear to return to his duties?"

"His duties?" Rex shifted his weight to better study Lord Audley. "Assuming he avoids any infections in his leg, Clark should be home within the next couple of days. As for how long it will take him to be back on his feet, I couldn't say. Why do you ask?"

Lord Audley glanced at his desk and then lifted his gaze but fell short of meeting Rex's eyes. "I thought I might take a holiday, but I did not want to go until Rivers is back to full form."

"A holiday?" Rex reared back, his brow full of wrinkles. "To the seaside? You, sir?"

"I am owed a brief reprieve from my responsibilities as much as the next man is," Audley retorted, looking somewhat put out.

"It is just, well..." Rex struggled to find the right words. "I have never known you to take time off. Dora has never mentioned you taking a break, either, and she has been in your employ for half a decade."

Lord Audley huffed, but his shoulders soon dropped back to their normal position. "I have never had someone to stand in for me. Someone who I trust implicitly. What better way to show this than by allowing the man time to stand on his own. Besides, I am reminded I have a nephew who will one day inherit my title. I can only imagine what his wastrel father and doting mother have allowed him to become. It is long past time when I should take his education in hand."

Rex pictured Audley walking along a pebbled beach with a young lad at his side. In his imagination, Audley still wore his bespoke suit, vest, and a stick pin in his lapel. The boy wore short pants and was barefoot. The resulting image was so absurd that he locked it in his head so he could share it with Dora later.

He wiped his hand over his mouth to hide his smile and issued a stern warning to pull himself together. Audley's little holiday was a rather momentous occasion, one which he might cancel if he thought it made him look a fool. The esteemed duke was far from a fool. Rex thought he just might be the smartest man in England.

Clark was not far off. He was young still, in comparison, and time would bring a wealth of experience. His sharp wits would stand him in good stead when it came to making future decisions.

As for Rex and Dora, Inga and Harris, and the other members of their household, they would go where life and country needed. After so long a stretch on England's shores, they were overdue for a trip to parts unknown. Oh, they would stay put long enough to see Clark back on his feet. But espionage and invaluable secrets waited for no man.

"One last question, Lord Rex, if I may," Audley said,

bringing Rex back to the present. "How is Miss Adams holding up?"

Rex's jovial expression fell to the floor, taking his idle thoughts with it. "She stayed with Clark until he reached the hospital but left as soon as she heard he came through the surgery."

"I see." He steepled his fingers again and tapped them against his chin. After a long moment of silence, he offered a suggestion. "Have Dora give her a ring. It is long past time she and Rivers stopped dancing around one another and instead attempted a two-step together. Figuratively, that is."

Rex's mouth dropped open. How and when had Lord Audley cottoned on to the burgeoning interest between the pair? Surely neither of them had turned to him for advice.

"Rex," Audley said. "The role of the spymaster is to know all the secrets. You and the others would be wise to keep that in mind. Especially once Rivers comes fully into his own."

Egads. That was a terrifying thought.

Rex limited himself to a nervous smile and promised to speak with his wife about that telephone call. After that, Audley called the butler back in. The man arrived bearing Rex's coat and hat, making clear the notice that his time with the duke was at an end.

For today, at least.

But not forever. Rex and Dora still had many adventures in front of them. But first, they had to make a call.

Chapter 24
Prudence Makes Her Move

Prudence fussed with the belt around her waist, uncertain whether it should be so tight. Once again, her reflection showed a young stranger. Certainly, the pretty woman wearing the chiffon day dress that emphasised her narrow waist could not be Prudence Adams.

The urge to rip the dress off and put on one of her old favourites nearly overwhelmed her. Who was she kidding?

No. I am doing this for Clark. So he will see me the way he did that night at the 43.

Not like that night months earlier in the library. When he'd kissed her until her mind ceased to spin tales and went quiet. But then that clap of thunder had made him pull away. She had not missed the horror that pulled at his features.

How could he, the newly minted Earl Rivers, possibly be happy with someone so... common?

But she wasn't common, she reminded herself. She was the niece of a member of the House of Lords. She, too, had grown up in the swirling lifestyle of the English ton, and what was left of it after the Great War. She had hated every minute of it.

Judged them all so harshly, until Dora, Rex, and Clark forced her to see below the surface.

She had been such a fool. How could she paint them all with a single brushstroke, yet demand they see her as someone different?

She forced her hands to still, her arms to relax until they hung at her side. She took another glimpse at the mirror. She wasn't up to Dora's standards, but then, who was? She hoped desperately that she was good enough for Clark to reconsider his interest in her.

He had almost died. Or he could have, had that gun pointed higher up. She had held a towel to his bleeding leg and prayed and prayed as her parents had taught her. She lost them at far too young an age. She could not lose him too. Even if he wasn't quite hers.

She turned around and marched out of her bedroom before her doubts could rise again. She grabbed her handbag and coat from the peg near the door and kept right on going. Going and going until she stood in front of Clark's stately townhouse on Curzon Street.

She would ring the bell because Dora said Clark wanted to see her. That he had asked about her. Dora had not ended their call until Prudence had promised to drop by Clark's home and pay him a visit.

Drat, the woman was insistent. Prudence supposed that was the secret of how darling Dora got so much accomplished. She simply refused to hear any answer other than the one she wanted.

The Georgian house loomed large, its four floors towering over the pavement. Weathered Portland stone graced the facade with an air of timeless sophistication. Large sash windows, framed by intricate iron balconies, reflected the golden glow of the morning sun, while the glossy black front door, adorned with a polished brass knocker, beckoned visitors into the realm of Mayfair's elite.

It beckoned her, as well. Her feet carried her up the walkway. Her hand raised the knocker once, twice, three times.

The man who answered was far too young to be a butler, yet he wore the proper attire. "May I help you?"

"I am here to see Clark, that is, Lord Rivers. If he will see me..." She was babbling. To the butler!

"Please, come in. I believe his lordship is expecting you." The butler stepped aside, opening the door widely in invitation. He beckoned her to follow, leading her along marble floors, deeper into the house. She watched his feet, too nervous to so much as glance at what must have been impressive decor.

"My lord, you have a visitor." The butler moved into the room, expecting Prudence to follow. She took a deep breath to centre herself and followed.

They were in a private sitting room, one with a rather feminine touch. Floral wallpaper, a bright yellow rug, and a basket of knitting proclaimed this to be the previous lady's domain. The reason Clark had chosen it today was obvious. He sat in a comfortable wingback, with his leg propped on a stool and a quilt keeping him warm. Sun shone through the tall sash windows that offered a view of the manicured gardens.

"Prudence?" Clark blinked several times. "You've come. Can you stay? For tea, that is? Is it too early for tea?"

Now which one of them was babbling? Prudence took courage from the admiration in Clark's gaze. Despite his first appearance as an invalid, his colour was high, his moustache waxed to perfection, and his white shirt revealed broad shoulders and a firm chest.

"Tea would be lovely, thank you." She chose a chair opposite him, so he would not have to turn to look at her. It kept them far apart, but perhaps that was for the best. "How are you?"

Clark flashed his trademark smile and reassured her that he was recovering well. They kept up the inane chatter—about the weather, the daily news, Rex and Dora—until a maid delivered the tea tray and poured them both a cup. She left the pot and a plate of iced biscuits on the table within easy reach of her master.

Prudence wrapped her hands around her porcelain cup, suddenly reminded of how cold they were. How nervous she was.

Clark, she noted, did not even lift his. He fiddled with the edge of the quilt, a habit she knew came from nerves. Why was he nervous? Her mind raced as she raised and discarded theory after theory.

"Prudence?" Clark's voice was hesitant as he said her name. "I wondered..."

"Yes?"

"Not soon, of course. Not until, well, you know..."

Prudence most certainly did not know. Soon, she should leave? Keep her distance? Move on?

"Would you like to go out to dinner?"

Prudence blinked her eyes, sure she had misheard. Dinner?

"Err, that is, only if you are free. We can invite along Dora and Rex. Perhaps some others. Make a night of it..."

Was Clark asking her to step out with him? The realisation that he just might be shot through her like a bolt of lightning splitting a tree in the village green. The doubting, hesitant, fearful half of her tore away, leaving behind only hope and promise and an overwhelming desire to say yes.

"I would love to go. With you, that is." Prudence allowed the delight coursing through her body to show on her face. "We needn't bring along the others."

"Are you certain?"

"I am." Prudence stilled. "Are you... uncertain?"

"I'm not uncert— oh blather, I am making rather a mess of this, aren't I?" Clark bore such a chagrinned expression that Prudence had to laugh. "I have wanted to invite you out for ages, but I was too afraid you would say no. I just, I couldn't face that."

"Why would I have said no?"

"Your face, that night, and then, you were so cold to me, and it was as though our time together never happened. It was all my fault. I was nowhere near worthy of you. I understood. That is why I worked so hard to show you I am serious about taking on more responsibility. Of stepping into Audley's shoes. And well, I thought maybe now, after all that happened, I would be a fool not to make the effort."

The world turned again, like the kaleidoscope her parents gave her one Christmas, the colours shifting to form a new pattern.

"But I thought you regretted it!" she insisted. "You could not get out of the library fast enough."

"You wanted me to stay?" His voice carried such anguish that Prudence's heart skipped a beat.

"I wanted to stay, with you. But what would the worldly Lord Rivers want with boring old Prudence?" Prudence shook her head at the both of them. "We are utter fools, you know. Dreadful, timid fools. Why didn't we discuss this before?"

Clark held out his hand, beckoning her to come closer. Prudence gathered her courage and rose from her chair. She crossed the room and sank down onto the chair beside him. Clark wiggled his fingers, not relenting until her palm rested against his. He laid his other hand on top, taking care not to put too much pressure on the gauze covering the burn he sustained.

"I don't want to go to dinner some night in the future,

Prudence. I want you to stay now. To have tea and dinner with me. To come back tomorrow for lunch and straight on through until it is so late, I have to send a footman to escort you safely home. Time is more precious to me than ever, and I do not intend to waste it."

"But your work," she said, though she didn't really mean it. "My work."

"We'll do our work here. I have a typewriter. I will get another. If you want, I will hire a secretary to take dictation." Clark squeezed her fingers. "Stay. Please."

There was such hope in his voice, but it was the edge of fear that convinced her he spoke the truth. He cared, desperately, about her answer.

"What will the neighbours say, Lord Rivers?"

"They will say that the new earl has lost his fool head over a dame and that it is about time he settles down. And then they will come round to see for themselves, and to congratulate me on my excellent taste. Though, they will not think so highly of you, my dearest."

"No?" Prudence tilted her head. "Whyever not?"

"Because you have allowed yourself to be swept off your feet by a known scoundrel. You have lowered your standards so far, they are dragging on the proverbial ground. Someone as clever and gorgeous and kind as you could have any man in the world."

"But she wants this man." Prudence gathered up her courage and leaned forward, until their lips were inches apart. Clark closed the gap.

* * *

As the writer of this tale, I would love to tell you that these two new lovebirds lived peacefully ever after. But we're talking about Clark and Prudence, a classic case of opposites attracting if I've ever seen one. Their future holds plenty of romance, punctuated with explosive disagreements, some of which happen simply to provide them with an excuse to make up.

Lord Clark can hardly be expected to behave for the rest of his days. And Prudence isn't going to bite her tongue if he steps out of line. But something tells me that they won't ever forget the core truth at the heart of their relationship. No one else on the planet sees the real them, and loves them for it, rather than despite it. Ups and downs will come, but maybe that is the right happily ever after for those two, after all.

* * *

Need something new to read? Discover my new historical mysteries - the Crown Jewels Mystery series - where intrepid duos solve crimes at the highest levels of Regency society.

Book 1: THE MISSING DIAMOND

In Regency London's glittering ballrooms, a well-made match can mean the difference between power and ruin.

London, 1813: With his reputation and inheritance on the line, Lord Percy is determined to win the heart of the coveted diamond of the season. When that beautiful woman vanishes, his failure seems all but certain.

Unless, that is, he can find her.

Lady Grace is devastated when her best friend disappears. Society may be willing to believe the worst, but Grace knows her friend would never run off without leaving her a clue.

Someone kidnapped her - but who?

With the clock ticking, Lord Percy and Lady Grace find

their best hope lies in working together. But strong wills, brash decisions, and pesky sparks aren't the only things standing in their way.

Can they trust each other in a society where people will do anything to rise to the top?

Find out in **The Missing Diamond**. Order your copy now on Amazon.

* * *

Want to keep updated on my newest books? Subscribe to my newsletter for book news, sales, special offers, and great reading recommendations. You can sign up here: lynnmorrison. myflodesk.com/dcd-newsletter

Historical Notes

The Red Scare of 1924

Nowadays, we are taught to be constantly on guard against fake news. The proliferation of technology, artificial intelligence, and dirty money makes it all too easy for the average person to swallow a lie. For anyone who thought this a modern phenomenon, I have bad news.

While researching the major events of 1924, I stumbled across a story about the so-called Zinoviev letter. Four days before the General Election in October, 1924, the Daily Mail ran a horrifying headline. It claimed to have intercepted a letter between Grigori Zinoviev, head of the Bolshevik propaganda organisation, and the British Communist Party. The letter called on the communists to connect with "sympathetic forces" in the ruling Labour Party to support a loan to the Bolsheviks (among other things) and to encourage "agitation-propaganda" in the British armed forces.

A vote for the Labour party was a vote for the communists... or at least, that is what the Daily Mail claimed.

The Labour Party, led by Ramsay MacDonald, called foul on the article. They said the letter was a forgery, and it was part of a smear campaign by the right wing. Their cries were not enough to save them in the election. The first Labour government fell with hardly a whimper, and the Conservatives retook the seat of power.

It took investigations in the 1960s and 1990s to unearth the truth. MI6 sources forged the letter. MI6 leaders then leaked it to the Conservative party, at a time likely to result in the most damage to the new Labour party. Gill Bennett, chief historian at the Foreign Office, conducted an exhaustive search of the MI6 archives. She concluded that the campaign was the work of officers with close ties to the Conservatives, and not an official activity of the organisation itself.

Needless to say, I found this tale fascinating, not the least because 2024 has seen the first Labour government come into office since 2010. Indeed, this is proving to be a year packed with consequential elections that could change the world order. One can certainly understand the desire to tip the scales, especially when your preferred party is at risk of losing. However, fair and free elections exist for a reason.

I took inspiration from the Zinoviev letter to craft a different tale, although I kept the major players the same. It was an interesting exercise to see how the story might change depending on who was pulling the puppet strings and why.

If you are interested in learning more about the Zinoviev Letter scandal, you might start with this article from The Guardian (https://www.theguardian.com/politics/1999/feb/04/uk.politicalnews6). If that whets your appetite for more, you can continue on with Gill Bennett's book on the topic: *The Zinoviev Letter: The Conspiracy that Never dies*, published by Oxford University Press in August 2018.

About Earl Rivers

Given Clark's larger than usual role in this book, I thought you might be interested in hearing about the history of his title.

When creating his character, I chose to use an extinct title. Earl Rivers as a peerage was first created and awarded to Richard Woodville in 1466. To quote from Wikipedia, "As borne by the Woodvilles, the title was not derived from the name of a place, but from an ancient family name, Redvers, or Reviers..." The Woodville line ran out in 1491, and the titled disappeared with them. It returned again, with a new 1st Earl Rivers, in 1626, and changed into Countess Rivers in 1641, as a title strictly for use by Elizabeth Savage, Countess Rivers, during her lifetime.

In 1776, the Baron Rivers title regained use and was awarded to George Pitt. If that name sounds vaguely familiar to any visitor of Oxford, England, there is a reason. The Pitt-Rivers line left their mark on the town and university, in the form of the Pitt Rivers Museum, founded by Augustus Henry Lane Fox, from 1880 known as Augustus Pitt Rivers, Lord Rivers.

You can find out more about the history of the Pitt Rivers Museum (a thoroughly fascinating institution) on their website: https://www.prm.ox.ac.uk/history-museum

Acknowledgments

Thanks to my dad, Ken Morrison, and my dear friend (and often co-writer) Anne Radcliffe for providing feedback and edits on this book.

As always, I am so grateful for the time and effort my beta readers—Brenda Chapman, Ewa Bartnik, Anne Kavcic—provide. They deal with my grammar snarls and plot holes without complaint and provide great feedback to make the end book better.

Thanks to my ARC team (especially Lois King and Joan Newman) for helping find any remaining pesky errors and get out the word about my books.

A final huge thanks to you, my readers! So many of you lend me support via email or comments in my Facebook group.

The Missing Diamond
A Crown Jewels Regency Mystery

In Regency London's glittering ballrooms, a well-made match can mean the difference between power and ruin.

London, 1813: With his reputation and inheritance on the line, Lord Percy is determined to win the heart of the coveted diamond of the season. When that beautiful woman vanishes, his failure seems all but certain.

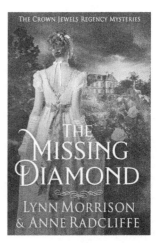

Unless, that is, he can find her.

Lady Grace is devastated when her best friend disappears. Society may be willing to believe the worst, but Grace knows her friend would never run off without leaving her a clue.

Someone kidnapped her - but who?

With the clock ticking, Lord Percy and Lady Grace find their best hope lies in working together. But strong wills, brash decisions, and pesky sparks aren't the only things standing in their way.

Can they trust each other in a society where people will do anything to rise to the top?

Find out in **The Missing Diamond**. Order your copy now on Amazon.

About the Author

Lynn Morrison lives in Oxford, England along with her husband, two daughters and two cats. Born and raised in Mississippi, her wanderlust attitude has led her to live in California, Italy, France, the UK, and the Netherlands. Despite having rubbed shoulders with presidential candidates and members of parliament, night-clubbed in Geneva and Prague, explored Japanese temples and scrambled through Roman ruins, Lynn's real life adventures can't compete with the stories in her mind.

She is as passionate about reading as she is writing, and can almost always be found with a book in hand. You can find out more about her on her website LynnMorrisonWriter.com.

You can chat with her directly in her Facebook group - Lynn Morrison's Not a Book Club - where she talks about books, life and anything else that crosses her mind.

facebook.com/nomadmomdiary

instagram.com/nomadmomdiary

bookbub.com/authors/lynn-morrison

goodreads.com/nomadmomdiary

amazon.com/Lynn-Morrison/e/BooIKC1LVW

Also by Lynn Morrison

Made in the USA
Coppell, TX
24 July 2025

52309285R00121